MARYAM SHUMATE
CHASED BY A BALLER

This is a work of fiction. Names, characters and incidents are products of the author's vivid imagination. Any resemblance to actual events, locales or persons, living or dead, is entirely coincidental.

All rights reserved.
No part of this book may be reproduced in any form or by any electronic or mechanical means including information storage and retrieval systems, without the written consent of the author, except for the use of brief quotations in a book review or a blog post.

DEDICATION

This book is dedicated to those who dream awake, those who refuse to quit after a setback and those who believe in the power of love. Love conquers all.

PROLOGUE

With two adorable kids, Onyeche decided to take a trip to a city in California. This was her first trip after her divorce and she was not overly excited but something in her seemed to be calling the shots and it seemed as though the more she tried to ignore the pull to take the trip, the harder the pull within her to take it.
After the divorce, she desired to give herself and her children a healthy life of fun memories and adventures. Little did she know that destiny was about to play a role in their lives. Whilst she planned this trip, she couldn't help but wonder about what was next for her and her kids. She had forgotten about what it felt like to care for herself because her life had been about her ex and her children. Something about the air of freedom from negative energy makes her feel like she could achieve anything and she intends to enjoy that feeling. Somehow it feels like she is ready for something new and different. Although she didn't know what that was, she wasn't stressed out about it.

When they arrived at the airport in California, she noticed the game ads displayed all over the airport. There was a huge football game that evening and she noticed all the ads had the picture of the star quarterback on them. He looks like a Greek god in his uniform and in one of the ads, they had him dressed like a Greek god holding a golden sword in one hand and a football with the other hand. He was also wearing a white robe with gold embroidery around the neck and midsection areas and a gold crown on his head. Whoever came up with this ad must have received inspiration from the gods because he looked the part. His eyes were a piercing grey and it felt like they were looking straight into her soul. While she stood there staring at this magnificent picture of him, something about it held her right there. She couldn't quite describe what it was that kept her attention on the picture.

"Mama, is that Kallie Goodall?" asked her 6 year old son. He knows his football players. "I don't know, son," she answered. "Can we go now?" He asked. "Yes, baby."
While they walked to their luggage, she couldn't stop thinking about those piercing grey eyes and perfectly defined abs. There was definitely something different about that experience for her.

After picking up their luggage, they located their uber driver at the entrance, right next to the international check in kiosk. She was excited that she made this trip. She had booked a really nice hotel for a week. She had read the reviews and was really happy with her choice. "It would be nice to really unwind and enjoy a different scenery and city with my kids," she thought to herself. I have heard that this city is a big football city and if you want to have a feel of the city, you have to go to a game. The game is tonight and I doubt that I could get a ticket this close to a game. Dear Lord, please make a way for us to have tickets to the game," she prayed. It would be nice to go to a game in person again. The Lord knows it has been a while since I last saw a game in person.

"Oiza, would you like to go to a football game tonight?" She asked her son. "Yes! I would love to go. Mama, are you taking us to see Kallie play?" He added. "I don't know yet but we will need to get tickets first. Tickets are sold out this close to the game but there's nothing God cannot do," she added. You and Oremeyi should pray to God to grant us three tickets to see the game tonight.
"Dear God, please give us tickets to the game tonight so we can

watch Kallie play, in Jesus Name. Amen!" The kids prayed in agreement. "AMEN!" Agreed Onyeche.

After the football game that night, her uber didn't show up as planned. While everyone was leaving the stadium as fast as their vehicles would allow them, Onyeche and her kids wandered around the stadium, hoping to spot a cab or have another uber respond to her search. As she was about to get frustrated with the whole situation, a very expensive looking sports car slowed and parked right beside them. When she turned to look, the driver's window rolled down. Before she could turn to see who it was, she heard "Hi Kallie, nice to meet you," greeted her son. When she turned to take a closer look at the stranger, who had just parked right where they were, she could not believe who she was about to come face to face with.
It all happened so fast, because he had already come out of his car and was standing right in front of her with a smile on his face and a hand stretched out to meet her.

20 MINUTES EARLIER IN THE LOCKER ROOM

Coach Wells

Hey everyone, I need your attention here. Let tonight's game be a lesson for all of us not to take any team for granted. We almost got our asses kicked by a team that hasn't played well in over ten years. I hope that we all have learned from this game because we almost lost a game that should've been a blowout. Thanks to Kallie's sixth sense with only a minute to go in the game and Julio's athleticism to out jump the defense, we narrowly took the W. So guys, let this be a lesson to our offense, defense and special teams, not to let up until the game is over alright? "Yes Sir!" The team responded in agreement.

As the players got ready to leave the stadium, Kallie was stopped by his linebacker; Hoggs. "Hey Kallie, I think the media is waiting for an interview from you. How are you going to explain the mess we almost put ourselves in? Asked Hoggs with a smile. "I'll just explain it as best as I can Hoggs," answered Kallie. "One more thing man, would you like to go to a private party with me and Jo? I heard one of her friends is throwing a really lit party and there'll be a lot of hot single mamas at the party," said Hoggs. "No man, I am too tired to go to a party tonight. Enjoy the party, Hoggs," responded Kallie as he declined the invitation with a smile.

Media Room

As Kallie made his way to the media room, he knew what was coming. There is going to be a lot of gossip about how the team needs a change, Kallie's contract may need to be re-evaluated and a possible look into the future with a more promising Quarterback and all that nonsense. "Right now, I have no time to worry about dumb stuff. I can't control what the media does or says but I can control how I respond to them," thought Kallie.

Kallie decided to keep his responses short and to the point as always. The journalists do not really like interviewing Kallie for this reason. He never entertains small talk with them.

Jim from The Sports Network

"Hi Kalli." Hello Jim, replied Kallie. "Kallie, we all saw how your team almost lost to a team that hasn't played better than a rat in ages. How do you explain that?" Well Jim, the team may not have played better than a rat in ages but they are still an NFL team. That means they play to compete too and they came out ready to compete with us today. We just kinda took them for granted based on their past record, which was a bad judgement on our part, but I am glad we quickly re-evaluated and made some good runs that gave us an edge," responded Kallie

Roach from Sky Sports

"Kallie, I saw a little limp from you when the lineman tackled you in the fourth quarter, did you feel like you could have continued playing or did you at some point want to quit?"

Hi Roach, being hit is part of the game and as a matter fact, I have been hit harder and still continued playing. So to answer your question, I didn't feel like quitting at any point during the game. I just had to take a break for the team's trainer to take a look at the ankle.

Riley from NFL Network

Hey Kallie, you looked good out there. What was going through your mind at the last minute of the game, when you were only up by 1 point? Because for a second there, it felt like the defense was going to get an interception and win the game."

"Well, Riley, just like you, I was on the edge and knew I couldn't make any mistakes. I also trust Julio. I noticed Julio was at the right spot and I slung the ball as high as I could to him because that dude is a beast. Not many people in the NFL can equal his athleticism. He caught the ball and scored a 15 yard touchdown for us to close out the game. That guy is special, I tell yah.

Media Coordinator

That's all the questions Kallie can take for the night. Thank you all for coming tonight. We will see you at the next game.

Random Reporter

"Hey Kallie, how is Chloe the girl we saw you kissing at Palm beach a week ago?"

As Kallie made his way out of the media room, he couldn't help but feel angry. He doesn't like the fact that the media has to follow him everywhere he goes, looking for things to write about him and the humiliation of being photographed wherever he goes just makes it hard sometimes to deal with.

"I know I signed up for this and part of being a star athlete is dealing with media pests," thought Kallie. Chloe has since moved on after setting me up to be photographed by the media. It seems like almost every girl I take an interest in is trying to get media famous through me. I would really like something real. I want my own family, a woman who is for real and wouldn't mind coming to my games and also doesn't care about media fame. Someone with great values and who wants a relationship of a lifetime. Does a woman like that even exist? I hope she does for my sake," wished Kallie.

KALLIE

He got into his McLaren 720s and started driving back to his hotel room. "Who is that gorgeous Queen with those two adorable kids standing over there? She looks frazzled like she missed her cab.

Present Moment

Hi there, do you need a ride? Pardon my manners. Hey little guy. I see you know my name. What's your name? "My name is Oiza and I'm 6 years old," responded Oiza. Nice name and nice to meet you Oiza. "Mom this is Kallie," Ozia introduced Kallie to his mom. "Hi Kallie, that was a really close game earlier but you did your magic as usual and pulled off the win. Congrats!" Said Onyeche. Thank you. What's your name? "Onyeche(ON-YAY-CH-AYE) and my little Angel over here is Oremeyi (O-RAY-MAY-E) and of course you already met my son Oiza," said Onyeche. Nice names, Onyichi and Orimiyi. "My name is not Onyichi, Kallie," said Onyeche with a smile.

"What are you doing here with your kids alone? He asked. "We were just stranded by our uber driver and I am trying to get another uber." Do you live in this town? "No, we don't, actually we are on vacation and today also happens to be our first day in this city and we decided to come to the game," she answered. Would you like a ride back to your hotel? "Haha Kallie. There is not enough room for an extra fly in your car," said Onyeche with

a smile.
Actually, I can go back and change my car for a bigger one if you give me a minute. Promise me you'll wait right here for me. "Okay, we will wait for you but please keep your word," pleaded Onyeche.

He got back into his McLaren and drove off to the parking lot as fast as he could before coach Wells left. "Hey man, I thought you left already," said coach Wells. Hey coach. I need a favor. Can I borrow your SUV for the night? "Sure. Is everything ok?" Yes, I just need it to give a friend and her kids a lift to their hotel. "Okay, sounds good to me and since this means that I get to drive your McLaren for a whole day," said coach Wells. "Here's your chance, coach. Please don't wreck my car. It's pretty expensive," he answered before he drove off in Coach Wells Yukon Denali.

"What is happening right now? How is this my life? Kallie the Greek God is giving us a ride," said Onyeche.

"Hi there. I'm back. Let me help get the kids in the car," offered Kallie. As they began to get the kids seated in the back seat of the brand new Yukon Denali, Onyeche couldn't help but admire how spacious and well crafted the SUV is. When they finished getting the kids seated, he asked her if she would like to sit in front with him and she said yes.
"What is the address of your hotel, Onyeche? "Wow! I can't believe you just said my name correctly," she teased. "The address is 123 Ocean Drive SF, 90251."
"I'm glad that made you laugh," he said then he entered the address on the GPS.

"Oh wait a minute, are you telling me you are at the Ocean View Hotel?" He asked, feeling excited. "Yes, that's where we will be staying for the next three days," She answered. She couldn't quite understand why he was so excited about her hotel. "What a coincidence! That is where I am also staying for the next few days. I am actually in the presidential suite and it has a lot of room in it. If you want to see what the presidential suite looks like, you are welcome to my room," he invited before evaluating what he sounded like.

"That would be nice but I don't think that it is necessary Mr. Kallie," she declined the invitation. "Oh please don't call me Mr Kallie, it makes me feel old. I prefer to be called Kallie."

"Oh I'm sorry Kallie," she apologized. "I am sorry if it sounded like my intentions were not pure, Onyeche. I didn't have any ulterior motives with that invitation. I am hungry, have you and the kids had dinner? "No, we haven't had dinner yet.

"Kids, are you hungry?" She turned and asked them. "Yes, I'd like some chicken," answered Oremeyi. How about you Oiza, are you hungry? "Yes, I'd like some food too, please. "I think it's right to say we are all hungry," she said, turning back to Kallie.. "Would you mind having dinner with me? I could use some company after such a close game."

"Sure, only if you promise to let me pay for dinner," She negotiated.

"Wow! You are definitely one of a kind. I'm supposed to be a superstar athlete whose net worth is spread all over the internet and major media outlets, yet here you are offering to pay for my dinner. Who are you and where did you come from?" He inquired. "Haha Kallie. I'm sure paying for your dinner is not a big deal. Moreover, you gave us a ride when our uber deserted us. Paying for dinner is the least I could do under the circumstances."

How could she be so confident and make light of an offer to pay for my dinner? This is the first time I have ever had a woman offer to pay for my dinner. All the women I've dated have always made it a priority to tell me that a man is always expected to pick up the tab but tonight is fast turning into something new. Maybe it's because she is married and is not expecting anything to happen between us. You know, I haven't even asked her about her relationship status. And I'm sure I didn't see a ring but maybe I'm wrong. Should I ask her if she is married or is it too soon? "Common Kallie, why do you have to overthink things all the time? You just met her," scolded his inner voice.

Hey, what time were you thinking of having dinner tonight? "Like right now because it is late and these kids are hungry," she responded.
"Oh my gosh! This sounds like we are a family," she silently thought with a smile.
I know the chef at the hotel and I'll ask him to make us something quick and delicious. Is there anything you or the kids are allergic to that I need to let the chef know about? "No, we are not allergic to anything but please make sure fish is not included because the kids would vomit on purpose if they smell or see fish," warned Onyeche. Okay, noted. Would steak, mashed potatoes, some roasted corn, carrots and some chocolate cake for desert work? "Yes! I love steak and the kids wouldn't mind it too," she said with satisfaction.

"Wow! I love how excited she got when she heard about the food. I Can't remember the last time I went on a date and actually saw a girl or woman get this excited about real food like this. Seems like most ladies these days care more about counting calories than actually enjoying a good meal with a man. I am really having an eventful evening and it only just started," he thought.

"Yay! Chocolate cake, said Oremeyi and Oiza at the same time. "Are you kids excited about dinner? He asked. "Yes we are," they answered. "It's the part about the cake that excites them," she said to Kallie and then turned to the kids... Oremeyi and Oiza, you'll both eat your dinner first before the chocolate cake. "Aww mama... Why can't we have the cake first?" They protested. "Because food is more nutritious than desert and that's it," she concluded.

"Mama, can I eat my dessert first before my steak?" Joked Kallie. Nope! You can't. Dinner first for everyone before dessert and that's final. "Yes, maam," he answered playfully.
There is something calming about Onyeche and this moment with her. Her spirit is beautiful and she is very beautiful too. I

love her chocolate brown skin and full lips. She looks good and slim. I love the curves on her body and how she moves her hands when she starts talking. Her hair is gorgeous. She is wearing a low cut and I can spot tiny curls in her hair. Her simplicity is so beautiful. Her makeup is minimal and her eyes are a tone of chocolate brown that almost look black when the sun shines in them. I have seen a lot of beautiful women but she is rare. It is almost like she is not aware how strikingly beautiful she is. I'm curious to find out if she is married because a woman like this doesn't come around often," thought Kallie.

On their way to the hotel, Onyeche couldn't help but wonder how this night had gone. Three hours earlier she almost changed her mind about going to the game but something within her seemed to have pushed her to take the almost free tickets that were sold to her by a woman whose date ditched her. The woman happened to be at the lobby when Onyeche was looking up last minute tickets to the game, on her phone. She doesn't remember if she had said her intentions out loud or if the woman had been snooping to see what Onyeche was trying to do on her phone. Anyways, it all turned out great because the price the lady sold her the tickets for was way less than what she was going to pay for them online.

Now, the star of the game is giving them a ride to their hotel and is also going to order dinner for them. "This is all so crazy good and all I did was set an intention to have a good time. Which sane woman would not want to have dinner with a gorgeous man?" She thought silently, with a smile. While she was still lost in her thoughts, she heard Kallie talking to someone over the phone.

"Yes, Chef Joe. Thank you. You're an angel. Onyeche and the kids will love you for this and you already know how I feel about you. You are the freaking best man! We will see you in a few minutes."

"Hey Kallie, was that dinner? I thought I heard you say the kids and I would love you," she asked. "You got it. That was the Chef and he happened to have made exactly what we wanted to eat. "That's amazing!" Sure is. Seems like God was looking out for us because he had made dinner for a family of four who had called last minute to cancel. He was wondering what to do with all that food when my call came in. He said maybe the food was meant for us after all. Weird but I believe God had us in mind when Chef Joe was cooking. He is the best Chef in the world and I always miss his food when I'm out of town.

"That's amazing. I am ready to eat a whole cow right now. I think I'm suddenly hungrier," she said and then yawned. We are almost there and from what Chef Joe told me, the table is ready in the conference room for us, as soon as we can get there. "Even better," She answered.
"Mama, are we there yet? I am very hungry," said Oremeyi. "Almost there baby. Mr Kallie is doing his best to get us there as fast as he can, okay? He has been kind enough to have his Chef make us something special to eat.
"We will be there in two minutes," announced Kallie.
The moment they turned into the hotel's parking lot, something in Kallie came alive. A feeling he has not had in a long time-- the feeling that the kind of family he's always wanted is finally real. For a long time he had been reminiscing on the idea of having a family of his own. Up until this moment, nothing in his relationships track record had seemed to include having a family. The girls he'd dated in the past seemed to care more about counting calories or giving interviews to celebrity magazines than about having a family. "Why did it take a random woman I happened to meet after a game to bring back a feeling I had taken a break from, for fear that it may never happen? He thought.

"We are here," he finally announced. Chef Joe is waiting in the conference room and he said he's set the place up like a party. From what I know about Chef Joe, I believe he went all out tonight. Hope you won't mind the display. "Oh Kallie, you and Chef Joe will make the kids' night and I don't mind that at all. Thank you for going out of your way for us tonight."

Oh I didn't do anything Onyeche. I somehow believe God

was looking out for us tonight.

As soon as Kallie parked the car, a valet came out to take the keys from him. Kallie waved at him to wait a minute because the kids needed to be helped out of the SUV first. Kallie reached for Oremeyi, while Onyeche reached for Oiza. Something about this activity made Kallie wonder how having his own family would feel like. "I can't wait to be a dad. I would be a really good dad and my kids would be happy that I am their dad," he thought silently. He handed the keys to the valet along with a tip of $100, and before leading Onyeche and the kids to the conference room where Chef Joe was already waiting with a big smile on his face. When the kids saw what Chef Joe had done to the space, they were so excited. There were balloons of various shapes and colors displayed on the wall and some on the floor.

There was also a bouncy house at the far corner of the room. It's location seemed intentional, like the adults wanted to create room for some privacy while the kids played. The kids' faces lit up and all they wanted to do was go jump in the bouncy house but their mom reminded them that they had to eat first.

"Awww mama," cried Oiza. "Mama can we please go jump first and eat later?" Asked Oremeyi. "My answer is a big fat no. You eat first and then play," she ordered.

Kallie watched while she was addressing the kids. The scene gave him a feeling of admiration for her and goosebumps. He loved how she didn't allow the kids to change her resolve. "I guess it's time to eat, everyone," announced Kallie. Could you all excuse me? I need to go use the men's room first and you can start eating without me. "Nope. We will go use the family restroom also. We have to wash our dirty hands and then come eat together," she responded.

"Okay, sounds like a plan," said Kallie, as he made his way to the men's room.

When she got out of the family room a few minutes later, she saw Kallie chatting with the Chef and he had a big smile on his face. He couldn't keep from letting Kallie know how happy he was that the food he had made would not go to waste.

"Hello Chef, thank you for such a beautiful creation. The dinner looks great and this decoration is second to none," she complimented. "Ohh my pleasure, my Queen and please make sure you enjoy it okay? Kallie here is like a son to me and I'll do anything to make him and his guests happy," he replied. "That is so sweet of you to say Chef. How much do we owe you for this? I already promised Kallie that I would pay for dinner tonight and I'd hate to see you go through the trouble and not be compensated properly for it," she said.

"Kallie, where did you meet such a sweet woman?" Asked Chef Joe, turning to Kallie. "She is amazing for real," he responded.

While Chef Joe was addressing Kallie, Onyeche dipped her hand in her purse and pulled out five $100 notes and handed them to Chef Joe. "I hope this helps cover dinner expenses."

Kallie immediately interrupted "Oh no! Onyeche, I didn't think you were being serious when you said you wanted to pay for dinner. Please keep the money and let me take care of Chef Joe." "Too late for that Kallie. I offered and I'm following through with it," she said with a smile and wink at him.

Chef Joe watched the exchange between them with a big smile on his face, while holding onto the $500 that Onyeche had just handed him. He thought how lucky Kallie was to have a generous friend like her. "How lucky is Kallie to have found a woman with such a generous heart," thought Chef Joe.

"I am done explaining myself Kallie, can we please eat now?"

"Okay but this conversation is not over and we have to talk after dinner," he said.

"Mr. Kallie, mama does this sort of thing all the time even for people she doesn't know. You won't win this one," advised Oiza.

The food was very delicious. The kids managed to finish their mashed potatoes and ate a little bit of their steak. Though they refused to eat their veggies, their mama didn't complain this time because Kallie was there. "Mama, can we go jump now? They asked. "You can go but please don't jump too high because you just ate," she advised. "Bye mama, see you later," said Oiza as he and Oremeyi made their way to the other end of the conference room where the bouncy house was waiting.

"I have never had this much fun with a total stranger with two kids until tonight. My night has been adventurous for sure but not like this. Leaving the game earlier, I was looking forward to a quiet night in my feelings because of how close we came to losing to a bad NFL team and of course the impending media backlash that would be unleashed on me and my team. But this moment, being here with you and how everything has gone, has been completely unexpected.

To be honest with you, I never stop to talk to strangers because the media would do anything to get a story on me, including setting me up. Knowing that, I always watch my back and make it my due diligence to only spend time with people in my small circle. I trust only a handful of people and they are mostly my siblings. Today, I broke my own rule and for some odd reason, I don't feel nervous about it. You give me a feeling of calmness like I have never felt before. Who are you and what are you doing in my city with your adorable kids?" He finally asked her with keen interest.

"Oh so intrusive," she said with a smile. "Are you always this intrusive with strangers or is it just with me?" She asked. I normally don't talk to strangers. You know, mama told me it is not safe to speak with strangers. But you, for some odd reason, don't feel like a stranger to me. "Oh really? How so?" I just feel it within me. "Who is to say that I am not an impersonator working for the paparazzi, who is looking for dirt on the Greek God Kallie?" She teased.

"Hahaha Greek God? I have been called many names but that one is definitely top of the list. Well, I know this may sound crazy and I get it because it does sound crazy to me too. But for some odd reason, I believe you are a great woman who didn't come with an ulterior motive towards me. I am going to take my chances with you. "Alrighty then. I guess it won't hurt sharing my story with you and If you try to use my story against me, I'll just deny ever talking to you and I mean it," she responded with a smile. "Hahaha I promise not to sell your story to the media," he joked.

"There's really not much to tell but I'll share it with you anyways.
You already know my name and that I am a mom of two babies whom you have already met. I am divorced. A few years back, I lost the drive to live for a while but kept pushing myself in spite of not feeling like living anymore. My ex was abusive verbally, mentally and emotionally but I did everything I could to protect my children from all of that toxic energy. I believe strongly in the power of prayer. So, whenever things would get dark around me, I would start praying to God to change the situation. Praying always made me feel good. The hope and energy I got from praying kept me strong for my kids. My ex did many things that I didn't approve of but never really addressed as much as I should have because I thought that just praying about it would change it and him.

Then one day, I woke up to a completely different person. He was erratic and threatened to kill me and sell my kids. He had a weapon in his hands and the only thing I could do was drop down on my knees and begin to worship God. I heard myself singing praises to God and got lost in it until I heard sirens outside the house. When I opened my eyes, the police were everywhere around the house. When I got up and opened the door, the police asked if I was okay and I said yes.

So they stepped aside and cuffed him and took him with them. The police called me the next day to give a statement about the incident. When I went in, I told them exactly what had happened. I told them he'd threatened to kill me and sell my kids. I asked the police how they got to my house so fast because I didn't remember calling them. They said they had received intel from someone who claimed to be close to him. The person had told them my ex had been threatening to kill me for a while and sell the kids. I asked them who it was that told them that but they didn't tell me because the person had asked to remain anonymous.

I was surprised as to how he might have reached that stage in his anger towards me but I am so grateful that the police came through the doors when they did. When I left the police station, there was only one thing left for me to do and I had to choose life in order to do it. I couldn't keep enduring a dead situation with my ex, I had to keep myself and kids safe apart from him.

I got a restraining order to keep him away from me and my kids. Though it has been an interesting road for me but it's been one that I know that I could never have made it through without my faith in God and I'm a strong woman," she said.
"Wow! I had no idea that you had to deal with all that. So sorry for having you relive such trauma," apologized Kallie. "It's okay. I'm alive and I have found my spark for life again. Look at me enjoying an exquisite dinner with the amazing one and only Kallie," Onyeche concluded with a smile.

"How did your friends and family react to the whole situation?" He finally asked. "Well, the pastor at the church I used to attend advised me to go and beg him to take me back, some close friends wanted to know if I was open to resolving the issue and others were happy my marriage was over. According to them, I was nothing without my ex," she replied, nodding her head with a smile.

"What?! Are you serious? The pastor asked you to go back and beg? That is really stupid of him. You know, I am really happy we met, Onyeche. You are an amazing woman and I know your kids are proud to have you. I see how happy they are and that bouncy house is really keeping them busy. It is so crazy that you and I met the way we did and I couldn't be more grateful that we met."

"Going to your game tonight was fun, the kids and I had such a great time and I'm glad I met you too. I had no idea that The Great Kallie would be our Uber driver and dinner host tonight, yet here we are."

While they finished their dinner together, there was an

undeniable magnetic connection growing between them. Kallie had been thinking about having a family of his own for a while but it seemed like all the women he'd met were only interested in counting calories and getting social media followers from their association. He doesn't consider himself unlucky in love but he knows he could use some help with the kind of women he attracted, until now.

There was once a time when he thought that family life may never be his path. Being a superstar athlete with lucrative brand deals and global attention from women and all kinds of people, there is always the projection from people about whom he should be with next. It's like random media hosts with nothing better to do, have taken it upon themselves to be his unsolicited matchmakers. They even predict how long each relationship should last until he and whoever they projected him to be with would move on to the next relationship.

He would rather not have the type of media attention that he gets but it comes with the role of being a great athlete. There are athletes who would do anything to get the kind of media attention Kallie gets but not him. He values his privacy.

Regardless of how hard the media tries to get an interview with Kallie they almost always fail. The only time they have access to speak with Kallie is during the preseason warm ups, while in training camp or after a game during the season. Another rare occasion that they get to interview him is when he partners up with a family brand that promotes education or valuable skills among young people. Other than these scenarios, the media doesn't bother him and during these occasions, he makes sure questions are about the cause he is promoting and nothing to do with his personal life.

He has the rare talent of being very present and intentional about everything he does. There are some very crafty reporters who have tried to rephrase their questions to get him to share something personal but Kallie always ignores those questions and makes it clear that his personal life is none of their business. His boundaries always leave the reporters frustrated each time.

ONYECHE

Oiza, Oremeyi, it's time to go. Mama is tired and needs a shower. "Awww can we please play some more?" They asked their mom. No, you can't. It is time to go and it is past your bedtime. You have been bouncing for over two hours and it's time to go," she ordered.
Kallie stood there witnessing the scene like this was his family. He feels drawn to them and doesn't understand why. "Can I walk you and the kids to the door of your room? I mean, I don't want to intrude but if you let me, I'd like to make sure you get to your room safely," he offered.

Haha Kallie, our room is not far away and you don't have to walk us up to it.
"I insist and please don't say no. Just give me a chance to complete an already amazing evening by walking my lady and her babies to the door. At least it's the best I can do after you paid for dinner," he pleaded.

Alright, if you insist and just so you know, I can take care of myself and my kids.

"I know you can and I also know that you are strong, independent and an amazing mom. I have no doubt you are capable of taking care of yourself but I insist on walking you to the door," he insisted.

Onyeche smiled and reached for her kids; one on each side as they walked out of the conference room to look for the elevators. SHe knew she couldn't get rid of him that easily. Not that she wanted to get rid of him but she wanted to show that she was more than capable of taking care of herself and her kids.

"Mama, I love elevators," blurted Oremeyi as they ran to the nearest elevator, which was a few doors away from the conference room. Kallie thought that he had had more fun tonight than any night he remembered. "How could a total stranger with her adorable kids bring me so much joy and excitement about my future?"

Kallie led the way to the elevator and before he pushed the button, he turned to her to ask what floor they were on? "We are on the 8th floor," she answered. "What? Are you serious? That is my floor too," he added with enthusiasm.

"Wow! What a coincidence, What's your room number?"

"It is 814 and what's yours?" he asked

. "It is 801," she replied.

"Mama we are here," announced the kids, as the elevator came to a stop at the 8th floor. "Well, here we are," she said. "Mama, can I open the door?" Asked Oiza. "Yes, baby. Here you go," said Onyeche as she passed the key to Oiza.

"Thank you Kallie for walking us to the door and thank you for giving us a ride back to the hotel and finally, thank you for an amazing dinner."

"No, thank you for giving me a great time tonight. It was a pleasure sharing the time with you and your adorable kids. May I please have your number now? I'd really like to stay in touch with you."

"No, you can't have my number but if you give me yours, I'll keep in touch," she responded. When Kallie heard her response, something in him dropped. It was a feeling of rejection that he'd not felt in a long time. He felt like she was getting rid of him and couldn't come straight to tell him. Of course he couldn't show his disappointment so she would not think he was a freak. No woman ever rejects Kallie but here's one that seems to be rejecting him. He is usually the one who picks and chooses his women and then moves on, most of the time. "This is so new and it stings and could this be how some of those women felt when I said no to them?" He thought silently.

"Ouch! That hurts,' he finally said out loud. "Are you alright? She asked.

"Yes, I just thought that it was okay if you gave me your number. I have no issue with giving you my number but I don't want you to not call me and then I won't have any way of contacting you," he replied honestly.

"Oh ok. Well, here's my number," she offered.

"Thanks and I just texted you. Please check and make sure you received it," he insisted.

Why am I being so clingy towards her? What is it about her that is drawing me to her and causing me to make a fool of myself? "I don't know Kallie," responded a still voice in his head. Maybe because she made you see how empty your life has been without a real connection. She has inspired you and given you a glimpse of what your future could be like," continue the still voice.

"If you don't mind seeing us again, we would like to invite you to breakfast with us in the morning," invited Onyeche.

"Hell yeah! I'd be delighted to have breakfast with you in the morning."

"Mama please come in. We are very tired and ready for bed," said the kids.

"Great! I'll text you at 7:00AM when we are ready to go"

"Sounds great. Good night, my lady and have a good night kids. I'll see you at breakfast in the morning," said Kallie before he finally walked away.

Are my babies ready for a warm shower? "Yes, please," they responded. Okay, I'll go start the shower now.

I finished giving them a shower and settled them in the bed for the night. Right before I got to doing my nightly meditations, I asked them to tell me about their day. Did you have a good day today? "Yes, mama. It was great. Thank you for showing us a good time mama," said Oiza. You are welcome. How about you, Oremeyi. Did you have a good time? "Yes, mama, the bouncy house was awesome," she responded.

Well, we all had a great day and even met a new friend. Are you both ready to say our nightly prayers now? "Yes, please,' they said. I led the prayer, gave them a hug, told them I loved them and turned the lights off.

As I watched my kids fall asleep, I began to think about where my life had been going a few months ago. My previous relationship with my kids' dad was unhealthy. He was insecure and judgemental. He always felt insecure each time I dressed up on our dates. In the earlier days of our dating he used to be so nervous when I would bring him around my friends. I had no problem bringing him along to see my friends because I loved him. Though my friends thought I could've done better but I didn't care because I was in love.

I embraced him in spite of his insecurities and subtle erratic tendencies. Well, it took a near death experience to cause me to change my resolve. Filing for a divorce and full custody of my kids was the best decision I could have ever made. If your spouse threatens to sell your kids and kill you, what would you do? I have asked this question many times and my answer is always the same.
Everything worked out for me and now, here I am in California with my kids, on a much needed getaway and of all the ways my day could've gone, I ended up meeting a superstar athlete; Kallie the Greek God himself. Dinner was great with him and I made sure I told him the gruesome part of my story either to scare him off or to let him know I am a strong woman who is not looking to make a great impression on him. I am looking to be me in all scenarios. I guess it's the mentality of a survivor.

A LOUD NOISE IN THE HALLWAY

"Hey Nicki, be quiet please. If you want Kallie to even consider you for a second, you have to act like you have your act together alright? Ordered Roger; Kallie's teammate. Roger had three girls with him that he intended to share with Kallie on their night of pleasure. He didn't even know if Kallie was into group sex but he intended to try his luck.

"What is that loud noise outside the hallway? Isn't it inappropriate for hotels to have parties in the hallways when guests are trying to sleep? I hope they don't wake my kids up because I would be very upset if they did," said Onyeche.

Roger and his guests didn't have any care in the world about other guests on that floor, as they loudly made their way to Kallie's door.

"Who is that? Onyeche is that you?" Asked Kallie as he made his way to the door. "Who the hell is Onyeche," asked Roger. "Oh! Roger, what are you doing here at this time? Hi ladies," Kallie greeted the ladies with an awkward smile, wondering why Roger was at his door with three women.

"Looks like Kallie has company," thought Onyeche, looking at Kallie's room direction. She saw one of Kallie's teammates, with three women spotting massive boobs. While they were making their way into the suite, he stepped aside, letting them in with a smile.

"I hope that they don't get too loud and wake up my kids tonight.

KALLIE

What is that loud noise outside my door? Is someone having a party in the hallway? I hope they don't wake up Oiza and Oremeyi because that would be awful. The kids need some good sleep. Oh wait a minute, when did I become so domestic talking about waking up kids? Wow! I don't know what is going on with me but oh well.
Is that a knock I hear at the door? While walking to the door, I heard the sound of a familiar voice. That sounds like Roger, but I hear other voices too and they don't sound familiar to me at all.

Hey Roger, I greeted as I opened the door to find out what he wanted. To my surprise, I saw him with three gorgeous women with massive boobs and before I could ask them to come in, they let themselves in and I had to step aside so they didn't move me out of the way. "Hey man, are you ready to party with us tonight? I brought you a gift and her name is Nicki," said Roger pointing at Nicki.

I don't remember ever asking Roger to hook me up with someone. I understand that my teammates do that sort of thing but I have never participated in it. I know how to get a woman when I want one and I have never asked Roger for help. This is so weird to me because this has a tone of orgy and I am not into that type of life. I looked at the girl that Roger said I could have and she was batting her extra long lashes at me. She looked ready for whatever they had planned for tonight but I was not ready for it. I pulled Roger aside to have a talk with him in one of the two living spaces I had in my suite.

"Hey man, I know we are pro athletes and orgies happen but I am not into this. Next time, please don't show up at my hotel without giving me a call first okay?," I warned.

"Common man! You need to loosen up for once. Nikki is gorgeous and amazing in bed. You would thank me later if you accepted my gift," said Roger. I appreciate the gift Roger, but I'll have to pass on it for now and for the future okay?

"Alright. Can you at least let us crash here for the night? It is too late for us to go home," pleaded Roger. Well, as much as I don't want to let you crash here, it's late and you can stay the night. There are two extra bedrooms in my suite. You and your company can share them. Please, keep the noise to a minimum because there is a family with kids a couple of rooms down the hallway okay? "Okay. Thanks man," said Roger with gratitude. No problem. Good night!

ONYECHE

Good morning sweet babies. "Good morning mama," answered Oiza and Oremeyi. Did you sleep well? "Yes, sweet mama. Did you sleep well too, mama?" They asked. Yes, I did. Who is ready for breakfast? "Me please," said Oiza. "I want biscuits, sausages, bacon and orange juice please," said Oremeyi. Baby, I hope they have what you want and if they don't we will still enjoy what they have okay? "Okay," Oremeyi answered.

Let's go brush our teeth before we eat breakfast. "Okay, mama," they agreed.

While we were brushing our teeth, I couldn't help but think about last night. I should say I couldn't help thinking about Kallie. He sure had an adventurous night. I think he might be too tired and preoccupied to join us for breakfast. Perhaps he may want to eat breakfast with his company instead of a single mom and her adorable loud kids. I'm okay with the change in plans that I am about to make. I won't text him nor will I call him. When we go to breakfast, if he shows up, I'll say hi but that is all there will be to it.

"Who is ready to go eat some delicious breakfast?" I asked my kids.

"We are!" They responded.

"Mama, are we using the elevator? My three year old asked. Yes, baby. Unless you want to do some serious exercise then we can go down the long flight of stairs. "No mama, I like the elevator," she clarified.

On our way to the elevator, my mind kept wandering back to Kallie. What if he and his guests catch us in the elevator? How would they react? I know I'll be fine because I have learned to think clearly with no hard feelings or awkwardness. I'm curious though to see how he responds to me after what happened last night. Did he even see me standing at my door when he moved aside for his guests to go into his suite last night? My life has been devoid of drama for a while, yet here I am creating one in my head.

"Good morning gorgeous," said a friendly looking bellman. Good morning handsome. Could you please show us to the breakfast area? "Sure, gorgeous. It is to your left from that huge Angel Michael statue," he directed. Thank you! "My pleasure. You have two beautiful babies," he complimented.

I thanked him as we made our way to the open dining. It was a breakfast buffet with everything beautifully arranged and in an orderly manner. The kids were excited at the sight of the food, as I was. They ate a little bit of their dinner last night and jumped on the trampoline for hours. If that's not enough to make them very hungry this morning, I don't know what else could.

"We are going to sit over here," I said, pointing at a table of four at a corner. "I'll place my purse over here so someone knows it is taken. Let's get some plates."

The breakfast buffett was beautifully arranged with a variety of breakfast choices. They had sausage links, paddies, cheese eggs, cold cereal, grits, fruits, french toasts, biscuits and gravy, butter, jelly, fried eggs, omelette and more. They also had a variety of juice to pick from. I got the kids' plates and loaded them up with biscuits, sausages and bacon.

Whilst we made our way back to our table, I couldn't help but notice someone familiar standing to the left of our table. He had a look in his eyes like he was looking for someone. As we got closer to our table, I registered who it was. It was Kallie. He looked very tired, like he didn't have much sleep last night. I wonder why he looks so tired. Not really. I don't want to bring myself to imagine what he could've been up to last night.

"Hey Kallie," greeted Oiza. "Hi Oiza. I was just looking for you guys," said Kallie with a smile. "I am glad you found us. Mama was just helping us fix our plates. Here, sit down, we saved you a spot," directed Oiza. "Thanks man, I appreciate it." Good morning Kallie. Hope you had a good night? I greeted him. "Good morning Onyeche. I apologize for being late to breakfast," he said. Haha you are not late to breakfast Kallie, we were just fixing our plates. Matter of fact, I need to go fix my plate now that I have the kids situated. "Please let me fix your plate. What would you like my lady?" He offered.

Oh thank you my wonderful man. I'd like two french toasts please, with a dash of maple syrup and some cheese eggs on the side, please. "Coming right up, Sugar," he said. I smiled and headed the opposite direction to get some orange juice for the kids. Thankfully, the fridge was placed a couple of steps from our table. I brought an extra bottle in case Kallie wanted some.

Having Kallie here feels great for some odd reason. It has been a while since I felt this calm around a grown man. He seems genuinely interested in me and my kids and that feels good.

"Here you go, my lady. Anything else for you?" No, I responded. He placed my plate in front of me and placed his plate down as well. I noticed he got some cold cereal and eggs for himself.

I am not even concerned that there might be a reporter hiding somewhere to take pictures of us for the paparazzi. This moment right here brings a fresh new hope that I will one day have the kind of man that brings joy and excitement to us. Though I am not really searching for one right now, I still want one. I know how it feels to have the wrong one and live each day with uncertainties and fear that something crazy might happen to you or your kids. Thank goodness, that is not how I live anymore.

Did you hear a loud noise in the hallway last night? I asked Kallie. "Yes, I did. When I first heard it, my first thought was; I hope this noise doesn't wake up the kids," he answered. Wow! I cannot believe that a stranger would care for my kids enough to think about them like this. "And it turned out that the noise was headed my way. My teammate; Roger, brought company with him and I had to let them spend the night because they looked too drunk to drive," he continued. "Yes, I saw that. I happened to open my door to ask the party to lower their voice right about the time you were stepping aside to let them in. I thought you all might have had an orgy," I teased.

"Orgy? Nope. That's not my thing at all. I don't know what came over Roger last night but I'm glad I was able to shelter them from a potential wreck last night," he said. "What is an orgy?" Asked Oiza. It is nothing you need to worry about, baby. I quickly responded to my son. "You look like you may need more sleep," I said to him. "I'm going to take a nap after breakfast. I couldn't sleep because Roger and his guests made my suite their playhouse last night. I was very glad they left early this morning. I was finally able to get an hour of sleep after they left. As soon as I woke up, I raced downstairs to catch breakfast with you. I honestly thought I would miss you this morning but here we are," he concluded.

While we finished our breakfast, I couldn't help but wonder why Kallie seemed so interested in me and my kids.

"What are you doing the rest of the day?" He asked. I plan on taking the kids to the zoo and the park afterwards. I heard the zoo here has some new exotic animals and the kids are excited to go and see them. "Oh! That sounds epic! Can I come with you?" Sure. If you don't mind the noise and mess. "I don't mind it at all. I actually love it." Okay, good. We are leaving at 12:30 PM. "I'll get the car ready. Is there anything you would need for yourself and the kids that I could bring?" Just yourself and the SUV. I have everything else handled.

"Mama, I am excited to see the Tiger at the zoo," announced Oiza. Me too, baby. It's going to be so much fun. "I want to see the penguins," said Oremeyi. Those are at the Aquarium baby. I plan on taking us there when we visit Atlanta soon.

KALLIE

Breakfast was really good and I found myself thinking about Onyeche and her kids. There is still a lot I don't know about her but still I feel drawn to her, like I never had before. Everything I have learned about her so far, gets me so excited and yet my rational mind tells me I must be going crazy. Something about our interaction makes me feel like I already have a family. I have always wondered about how life would be like calling my wife on the phone or going to her in the stands after a game. I have often wondered how it would be like having a wife and kids come to my home and away games.

Somehow, this encounter with Onyeche makes me feel like I am finally home. Yet there's still a lot I want to learn about her and questions I'd like to ask her.
Who in their right minds falls on their knees and begins to sing praise and worship songs when they are faced with death? Is all that even true? Would I need to hire a private investigator to do some digging for me? "You just met this woman, Kallie. Why bother going through this stress. You don't even know if she is open to dating yet. You don't know if her crazy ex husband is still in the picture. What would the media do if they find out you are interested in a woman with a complicated relationship history?" Interrupted his inner voice.

There may be a lot of questions with Onyeche, but I am open to learning more about her. It is so crazy that a few days ago, I was just thinking about what my life would be like if I had a wife and kids to go back to after a challenging game or a loss. It gets lonely sometimes not having a woman whom I can go back to after a hard game like yesterday. Onyeche feels like the kind of woman that would listen and support her man no matter what. A woman like this is rare and I have to come up with a plan soon. I need to ask her how much longer she will be in town and what her plans are for later.

As close as that game was last night, I'm glad I have not had to worry too much about it because at the end of the day a win is a win, no matter how ugly the game was. I still have to review the game tape to see my areas of weakness that I can work on for our next game. Knowing the NFL as much as I do, our next opponents are already busy coming up with a strategy to defend our offense and we have to make changes that will throw them off. Since our next game is not until next Sunday, I have a couple of days till we have to report to practice. How am I going to decide on this new friendship with Onyeche? What am I even doing? She hasn't even expressed any interest in me and I am already deciding her future? Common Kallie, get yourself together.

I picked up my phone and texted Onyeche. "I have the SUV and I am at the valet parking downstairs, when you and the kids are ready." I heard the beep on my phone and it was a response from Onyeche. "Thanks handsome. We will be there shortly," she said. Wow! She thinks I'm handsome and that's a good sign. Should I be happy now or scared? Is that a sign that she is interested in me? I wouldn't want to lead her on or have her lead me on either. "Calm down Kallie. You have to keep a steady head and not let your emotions steer you in a media frenzy," said a still voice to me. I decided to keep my cool to see how the excitement played out with my new make-belief family.

While I waited for Onyeche and the kids, I couldn't control my excitement about how much fun we have ahead of us. Why am I not even worried about the media seeing us and taking pictures? I'd better warn Onyeche about the possibility of a gossip column taking our picture and coming up with bogus stories about our relationship or lack of one. This reminds me of Rachael, the model I dated a few months back. She was gorgeous and l liked her but she wasn't really into me in the way that I wanted. She was more into building her social media following than she was about having me in her life. I remember taking her to this private Island for a two day getaway. A trip I had planned with so much excitement in the hope that we would not be disturbed and no news of us would be leaked. Well, it turned out Rachael had a plan of her own. Since I have always kept my dating life private, I intended to keep it that way but was utterly blindsided by her.

Rachael had made a deal with a magazine to leak photos of us to them for publicity, brand deals and to gain social media following.When I asked her why she had shared pictures of our retreat with the media, she said because she could. I had noticed that twenty four hours after she'd shared the pictures, her social media pages blew up and she was being contacted by all the magazine outlets to do an interview with them about our relationship. Of course she accepted their offer. I had advised her to keep what we had private but she said no. We broke up afterwards and she gained over 2 million new followers after that. It is so depressing to see the coldness in most people these days.

Seems like everyone is either looking for an opportunity to share something with the media that would cause their online presence to go viral or become social media stars, even at the expense of finding true happiness. Thinking about the incident doesn't sting as much now. After all, it is what it is and all I have to do is move on and hope the next woman I fall for is genuine and wants the same things and feels the same way about me.

Onyeche seems different in a lot of ways. She has kids and seems completely devoted to them. I have heard it said that you can tell a lot about a woman by the way she treats her kids. She has also not picked up her phone in the time I have spent with her. Her presence has been completely immersed in each activity we have been involved in so far. Her eyes are always on her kids and she seems like a mama bear ready to pounce on anything that threatens the safety of her kids and I think that's sexy. If she could be this way about her kids, I'm curious as to how devoted she could be to a man who proves to her that he is worthy of her attention and love. Something in me makes me wish I am he.

ONYECHE

Kallie is a good looking man and he seems genuinely interested in me. For a man who has such fame and notoriety, he seems completely at peace with having a family life. Something about the way he wants to be involved with me and my kids makes me feel at home in his presence. I have had my share of mishaps in relationships but something about this encounter with him seems different. Since my breakup, I have not sworn off men but I have been so committed to motherhood and my kids' needs that I haven't thought about dating again. Yes, I get horny sometimes, especially when I am ovulating but I have not felt the compulsion to go hunting for a man to have sex with until now.

Something about Kallie makes me tingle between my legs and expand within my heart. I don't know why I feel this way but it's probably because I have not let any man come this close to me until now. This would not have happened if it were up to me but Kallie seems genuinely interested in me and my kids. I hope his intentions are pure and I still feel weird around him because of how my body is reacting but I do have self control. I know better than to jump in bed with his sexy self. Besides, he has a game coming up in Boston in a few days. I'm sure he will be leaving soon and we will never see each other again. Whatever may be the outcome of this encounter, I am open to enjoying these moments with my children with or without a sexy specimen around me called Kallie.

Life has a way of turning out differently when you let go of all the heavy negative energy that no longer serves you. I shared the tough part of my experience with Kallie because that part would scare most people off. It seems like most people these days only want rosy stories. I however, love depth in an individual, because I have depth to me. All that I have experienced are memories of the journey that molded me into the person that I am proud of being today. Up until now, I didn't think I would care to want to know more about another man. Because I have kids and could live the rest of my life without remarrying but Kallie brings new sensations in me that gets me so excited about the possibility of having another man in my life.

I have watched him jump in front of my kids whenever it seemed like a stranger might bump into them. He acts like he is the kids' dad and that warms my heart. I plan on having an amazing day with the kids today while I make sure not to get in their way too much. Being a mom is a privilege that I don't take for granted. I have seen many moms neglect their children and place them in very vulnerable situations but that's not me. I always make it clear wherever I go that my kids are my responsibility and I will not tolerate crap from anyone that tries to mess with them. I am always ready to make sacrifices for my kids and if I ever remarry, I want a husband who is willing to make sacrifices for the kids too. I want someone who loves my kids and understands that I come as a package deal. What am I doing thinking about my whole life and future right now? It's not like Kallie has said anything about staying in touch or getting to know me after this soap opera we are having is over.

"Oiza, Oremeyi, please hurry up," I called out. Kallie is waiting outside for us. "I need my toy," said Oremeyi. Okay, go get it and let's go. I don't even see the need for that toy because we are going to the zoo and you might find something else you like while we are looking at the animals. Oiza, do you need to pee before we leave? I turned and asked Oiza. "No mama, I already peed," he responded, irritated at my intrusion.

KALLIE

Onyeche is one sexy mama. Can she tell that I am watching her as she walks towards me holding each child by her side? She looks really good in those blue jean shorts and yellow tank top. Her arms look toned like she goes to the gym. I look forward to enjoying this time with her and the kids. I have a big smile on my face as my new family walks towards me. Oiza ran and gave me a hug as soon as he saw me. I didn't know that he had seen me from a distance. "Hey buddy," I said as he jumped into my arms.

"Hi Kallie, I saw you looking at mama," he said. That statement made me blush because he was loud and his mom would've heard him. This kid is very watchful. "Your mama looks really good and I was admiring her outfit," I said. "Oh. I thought you were thinking about having us as family," Oiza added. "Whoa!" Who is this kid? I asked silently.

"Hello Kallie, you look nice today," greeted Onyeche. "Thank you," I responded with a big smile on my face, hoping she wouldn't notice my blush. "You look gorgeous in those shorts girl," I added. "Oh thanks. It's comfortable and I wanted to be able to chase the kids around," she said.

I hope you don't mind but I brought a picnic. "Aww Kallie, you didn't have to do that," she said. "I had plans to take us to one of the restaurants at the zoo to eat lunch," she explained. I thought that you and the kids wouldn't mind some fresh sandwiches and soups for lunch. I also packed some juice, nuts, fruits and chips. I didn't know what you wanted so I packed all I could. "You're so sweet, Kallie. Thank you so much," she thanked me. You are welcome and I don't mind doing nice things for people I care about. "Oohhh are you saying that you care about me and my kids?" She asked me. Yes, of course. Now let's get going before the zoo fills up and tickets are sold out. "I have a surprise for you too. I know it was last minute when you decided to come with us, so I got you tickets to the zoo," she said. Thank you so much, Onyeche. I was thinking about purchasing the tickets at the zoo but I'm glad you got them.

I'll help Oiza into his seat while you get Orimiyi," I offered. "Haahah Kallie, her name is O-RE-ME-YI. You make me laugh when you call her Orimiyi," she corrected me. God, I love seeing her laugh. I wish I could hear her laugh all day everyday. "I know how to pronounce her name," I said. I just wanted to make you laugh.

"Thank you for being so kind and for being helpful with the kids. You are truly one of a kind, Kallie," she said and then made her way into the front seat.

"It's my pleasure, Gorgeous," I added. God, I am so happy Coach Wells let me borrow his SUV. "This is the perfect family car," I thought to myself.

We got to the zoo and Onyeche brought her phone out and gave it to the guy at the gate who was more interested in checking her out than scanning the barcodes that she was stretching to him. I swear I felt like punching that dude in the gut for his intense look at my girl. Oh wait, why am I being possessive already? She has not even asked me about my relationship or life. All she knows about me is that I am Kallie, the one who almost lost the game for his team. I have to be open with her and let her know what I want from her. After all, I will be leaving for my next game in two days. She needs to know a little more about me and decide if she wants me to be a part of her life or not. Her reaction will tell me what I need to know and what I will do next.

She turned and handed me my ticket. I took it with joy because I am also a kid at heart. I love animals and I was particularly excited about the otters. They are so cute and they were recently brought from the Florida coasts to this zoo. Just for the otters, the zoo committee got funding and built an aquarium style habitat for the six special otters at this location. Haha aren't the otters such lucky bastards?

"I want to see the lions and tigers mama," blurted Oiza. "Don't worry baby, you'll see them today okay?"

"Mama, I want to see the monkeys and big cats," said Oremeyi. "You will see all of them today baby," she responded. I love how patient and attentive she is with her kids. I could just tell by the way her kids respond to her that they adore her.

We had been here at the zoo for about forty five minutes when my phone started buzzing off the hook. While I was reaching into my pocket to check on it, five huge cameras were suddenly in my face with reporters asking me questions and taking pictures. It was so annoying. The crowd was building up around me so fast and all I could think about was Onyeche and the kids. I ignored the reporters and headed to the swing where Oiza and Oremeyi were taking a break after walking around the zoo to see all the animals. As I walked up to them, I could see Onyeche's expression. She was wondering about what I was going to do. I walked up to her and asked her if it was okay if we left since the reporters and people were interrupting our peaceful afternoon. She agreed and we each carried a child and walked out. I didn't say a word to the reporters because there was nothing to say.

My concern was to make sure the kids and Onyeche were safe.

Being a star comes with its perks and downside and this was one downside. You become a target for unstable people and I didn't want to place Onyeche and her kids in harm's way because they mean too much to me.

While we were making our way out, I couldn't help but notice some reporters taking pictures of us. I was going to worry about what the headlines would be the next day but I chose to keep the thought off my head. "Thank you for protecting my kids Kallie. You are an honorable man. Your girlfriend must be so lucky to have you," she said. I couldn't wait to stop her. She thought I had a girlfriend but in all honesty, I didn't. It's crazy how she didn't act like she had read any of the nasty media posts about me. Who was Onyeche and why did she make everything so light and easy? I couldn't help asking these questions in my head. I made up my mind right there to find out all I could about her.

Hey girl, do you mind spending time in my suite this afternoon with the kids? I'd like to be in a safe and controlled environment with you and the kids. A place where we can talk and the kids can be preoccupied with stuff to do, so that we can get to know eachother better while they are busy. "Hmm I don't know about that. How big is the presidential suite and do you have a playhouse or something that can keep the kids busy while we talk?" She asked.

Well, I sort of already had that arranged. I had the urge to ask the event planning team at the hotel to add something that toddlers would like in my suite. Honestly, it is going to surprise me too because I have not seen what they did. I hope that the kids love whatever they did to the suite.

I reached out and grabbed Onyeche's left hand and said "I apologize for the way your time at the zoo went today. I wish we could have been there longer for you and the kids. Hope you are not mad at me?" I said with sincerity in my voice. "No, I am not mad at all. You did what had to be done and I commend you for that," she said while looking into my eyes.

I have been with many women but none has ever looked me in the eyes and expressed gratitude with such warmth and calm confidence like this. I have seen those who flutter their lashes and those who turn their face away in shyness but never one who looks me in the eyes and firmly shakes my hand without batting her lashes yet sends thrills throughout my whole body.

Who are you Onyeche and why do I feel like we belong together?

ONYECHE

I watched as Kallie made his way away from the prying reporters to me and the kids. He had a protective glare in his eyes that I wanted to see in my ex but never saw. He looked like a papa bear coming to protect his family from enemy attacks. When I saw that expression, I knew I would agree to whatever he suggested we did. I have heard rumors here and there about superstar athletes being arrogant and attention seeking but not Kallie. In fact, he ignores the reporters.

He is more interested in his craft than the media attention. Watching him protect me and my kids from the media mob today made me wonder why he is doing all of this. We just met last night and all he wants to do is spend time with us. I have questions I want to ask him and I am happy that the turn of events have opened the way for me to ask these questions. He just invited me and the kids to spend the afternoon in his suite. He even went to the trouble to make special arrangements for the kids. I hope the kids get distracted and preoccupied by the surprise in Kallie's suite and leave me enough time to ask him questions.

I would be a fool to think that he doesn't like me because I can read people's energy very well and Kallie does have feelings for me. Something tells me he is serious about having a family of his own. While we were driving into the valet parking, I couldn't help but notice how nervously excited Kallie was. "Onyeche, would you mind if I helped Oremeyi out, while you helped Oiza out of his seat?," he asked. I don't mind at all and thank you for doing this. "You're welcome. Wait right here Princess," commanded Kallie after helping her out and then reached for the picnic cooler. He held the picnic cooler in one hand and held Oremeyi in the other. I was surprised to see Oremeyi happily walk beside Kallie without getting upset. I know my baby girl very well. She doesn't like strangers, period. It surprised me to see how well she has taken to Kallie.

"Kallie, what have you done to my girl?" I asked. "What do you mean?" Oremeyi hardly lets anyone hold her hand except for me but look at you holding her hand and she allows it. "She is the Princess and I am the guide," Kallie responded with a smile. "Can I press the button on the elevator?" Asked Oremeyi as she raced to the elevator. I saw Kallie race after her with the cooler in one hand.

"Mama I'm hungry," announced Oiza. I need a sandwich and some juice," he cried. "Don't worry son, you are going to eat as soon as we get to the suite," responded Kallie. I watched Kallie take on the fatherly role and I couldn't help but be proud of him. I have had some experience with people forcing themselves into roles they have no business being in but not this time. With him, everything seemed natural and it was inspiring to watch.

Wow! Kallie, you went all out didn't you? Look at all these forts and that playhouse. "Anything for you and the kids, my lady," he responded. I couldn't stop myself from appreciating the setup in Kallie's suite. He had the design team arrange a 10 foot long fort that stretched from the living room to the connecting lounge area. It was quite the sight. He even had them place a bunch of gigantic stuffed bears and tigers on the corners. The kids truly had a lot of things to keep them busy that afternoon. It is unbelievable to have someone go to the struggle to make your kids happy, when you only just met them. Could this be God's way of paying me back for all I endured and went through in past relationships? Whatever this is, I am liking it.

Kids, can we eat lunch first before you go explore? "Awww

mama. Can we play first? We are not hungry," said Oiza, the self appointed spokesperson. Sure. You can play for thirty minutes and then we can have lunch. "Thank you mama," he said. You're welcome baby. "Oremeyi, would you like to eat first before playing? I asked, already knowing what her answer would be. "No mama. I'd like to play in the fort first." Alright kids, make sure you are ready to eat in thirty minutes okay? They both ran off not paying attention to anything I was saying. I turned to Kallie who was watching me and the kids with amusement in his eyes. Well thank you for distracting the kids from their food.

"Oh I didn't do anything but create a perfect atmosphere for you and I to really talk while you still keep an eye on the kids," he said. Okay, what do you want to talk about? "Well, I was hoping to talk about what we do after this place. Obviously we will both be leaving this hotel sooner or later and we will need to stay in touch after here. That is if you want to stay in touch of course. I don't want to assume that you want to stay connected with me after these encounters," said Kallie. You know, I have been thinking about that too. I have questions for you and I hope you really open up and share the answers with me. Do you have a girlfriend? "No, I don't have a girlfriend," he answered. Whew! Okay.

Do you have a side chick that you booty call when you are horny? "A what?" A girl you are not attached to emotionally but who you have an agreement with to come by whenever you are horny? "Oh man! You're straight forward with the questions aren't you? Well, since you asked. I did have a girl that I was seeing casually but we haven't talked in a long time," he answered. Are you going to be talking soon as I leave? "I don't know. I guess it depends on what you and I have going on," he answered honestly.

What exactly do you mean by "what you and I have going? "Well, I don't know if you have noticed but I have a crush on you. I don't know how this happened but I do. You make me want to be a part of your life. Prior to meeting you last night, I had been thinking about marriage, wife and kids. I want to experience all of that with a woman who is loving and caring towards me and our kids. All of the women I have been with until last night, none had expressed any desire to have a family and start one.

To be honest with you, I have never been with a woman who made me excited for a family like you. I believe that everything starts with a family and I would love to have my own sooner than later," he said. How does this relate to me? "Watching you care for your kids and pay attention to me while making sure your kids are protected makes me feel like my future might be right before my eyes and I may miss it if I don't act fast," he confessed. Your future? What do you mean by that? "Well, I find you very attractive and I think you are an amazing mom. I have never been this uncontrollably attracted to a woman before and definitely not one with kids until you. This is how strong the attraction is.

I am supposed to be reviewing game films in order to not repeat the same mistakes we made in last night's game but here I am talking to you. This may sound crazy but I think I may be falling in love with you already," said Kallie. Whoa! Hold up now. I am not going to have sex with you okay? If that is the line you want to pull in order to get in my pants boy, it won't work. "Oh no Onyeche. I am not trying to get in your pants, at least not right now. I am serious about how I am feeling for you. I didn't intend to express myself just now but something in me prompted me to let it all out," he continued.

This is definitely weird for me for many reasons. First, you are like the hottest man I have ever set my eyes on and also the kindest from the start and the richest and most popular and now the first to express falling for me this early. Are you sure everything is okay with you? Like are you sure you are not infatuated because my kids like you and I heard one or two people compliment you and us thinking we are a family? "No, it has nothing to do with any of that. Let me tell you something else. Before I met you last night, something prompted me to hurry and drive towards Gate D parking lot.

Since we started playing in this Arena three seasons ago, I had never driven by this Gate until last night.. When I saw you and the kids looking lost, I heard a voice say to me that's her. I may not be able to explain this well and I probably sound like a freak right now, but I believe I was guided to you," he concluded. Thank you for opening up to me. I don't believe that you are weird at all. I have seen and heard stranger things. I have questions to ask you. Have you ever dated a woman with kids before? "No, but I love my nieces and nephews and want kids," he answered. Have you ever spent the night in a home with kids before? "Yes, my nieces and nephews and their parents have spent holidays at my place and I often visit them too. I can't tell you how much I love the experience. Each time I am around them, all I think about is having my own kids and seeing them grow up together and play together," he explained. Okay, that sounds like you really know what you are talking about. Kids are loud and can be crazy and out of control sometimes. I want you to know that mine are no different.

       Anyone worthy to be in my life has to understand what he is getting into. I don't tolerate profanity around my kids and I protect them from any perceived danger. I guess what I am trying to say is that I won't choose a man over my kids if I am put in that position, my kids will always come first. I want someone who loves my kids almost as much as me and would protect them and accept them completely. "I can promise you that you have nothing to worry about with me. As you can tell, they already like me," said Kallie feeling proud of himself. They like you because of the surprises you have given them. I teased him.

KALLIE

Talking to Onyeche about my feelings is the right thing to do. I have never been this vulnerable before with anyone I just met barely twenty four hours ago. This feels different but I believe it is different for a good reason. Would you like me to get the kids so we can all have lunch now? "Not yet. Let's allow them to play a little longer," she replied. Okay. My turn to ask you some questions.

Are you and your ex on good terms? "No, I mean if someone tries to kill you and sell your kids, would you be on good terms with them?" She responded. Hell no. "I have forgiven the situation but won't create the space for me or my children to be hurt again," she continued. Does he come by to see the kids? Is he even allowed to see the kids? I asked to understand the situation. "Well, the cops have their eyes on him and he really doesn't care about the kids. He is more interested in getting high and partying than coming after me or the kids."

Wow! That's so sad that a man would treat a queen like you and his adorable kids with such disrespect.

"Honestly, I am grateful for everything. I no longer wake up afraid or wondering where our lives are headed. I have clarity and that is mostly because I gave the marriage my all even when I knew I was doing myself a disservice. Even though everything I did and gave was not enough, I have no regrets and my desire now is to give my kids and myself a better life.

I learned a big lesson from my marriage and that is to

always put me first. Since I let go of the heaviness and negative atmosphere, my life has been a lot better and I see things more clearly," she said. That's amazing, girl! I am so proud of the woman that you are. I am very excited to get to know you even more. So, where do you live? "I live in Colorado Springs." Oh really? "Yes. Do you know someone who lives in Colorado Springs?" She asked me. No, but I have heard stories about Colorado Springs and always wanted to visit.

See, now I have to visit because I know you. She laughed and it is always an amazing sight to see. Are you currently seeing anyone? Do you have a booty call boyfriend to warm your bed? Because it gets really cold in Colorado during the winter. I asked with a smile on my face. "No, I don't have a boyfriend nor do I have a booty call. I have been very busy healing from the patterns in my past relationship because I don't want to make the same mistake again. My kids' safety and peace mean a lot to me and that is why I am careful who and what I bring around us," she answered. Does that mean that I pass the test? "Sort of. With you, I'm still evaluating the situation and there is not much I can do when you're intentionally doing things to win my kids over. I just ask that you minimize the efforts and let things happen naturally,' she advised.

Okay ma'am. I will try to minimize it. "You better," she warned. My eyes drifted to her full lips and I couldn't help but imagine what her lips would taste like. "So, have you had time to think about your last game?" She asked. No, I have not because I have been too busy devising ways to win your heart to worry about my first love; football. I believe that's how you know you have found the one. "Why are you being so presumptuous?" She asked me. You are special and I am willing to make the necessary sacrifice to get to know you. "What would your parents think about you dating a single mom?"

My parents care about my happiness and would want me to be happy. Moreover, they will love you and the kids because you guys are so lovable. "What if they are not happy with it? What if their dream is for you to marry a woman who has never had kids so you could raise your kids together?" She asked like she is intentionally trying to scare me off. Well, if they don't accept my choice, they don't have to live with me. At the end of the day, it is my life and my choice. I don't want you to worry about a thing girl. My family would love you very much. "Okay. I think we should get the kids to eat now. Our conversation has made me hungrier," she said.

Oiza, Oremeyi come eat. Your lunch is ready." To my surprise, the kids came bolting towards me. They had played so much that they looked ready for a nap. "Did you guys have fun?"Asked their mom. "We did, mama," they answered.

    We ate our lunch together. I helped serve the kids and they expressed their gratitude. Onyeche was amazed at how well I did, serving the kids. "You are really a natural, Kallie. Thank you for treating my angels with such care and love." You are welcome. "Mama, can we go take a nap now?" They asked. "Yes, baby. Let's take you to our room," she responded, getting up. Onyeche, they can take a nap in one of the other rooms here. Housekeeping team already cleaned it up, changed the sheets and sanitized the room. The kids are welcome to take a nap in my suite, if you don't mind. "I do mind, Kallie," she protested.

    But I don't mind and I insist that you all stay here with me, please. I would really like to learn more about you, while the kids are asleep nearby. "I have never done this before either but okay. I'll go tuck them in now. I'll be right back, okay?"

    I'll be waiting here for you. She came out ten minutes later with a smile on her face. "You know, this is the first time I have ever gotten this close to a celebrity before and spent time in the privacy of his space," she said. Well, I may be popular and well known but I am still human too. It doesn't matter the fame and accolades or lies about me, at the end of the day, I am just a person. "Yes, you are," she agreed as she walked closer to where I was sitting. I could feel the air getting charged up with sexual energy between us and I tried hard to conceal my erection. Damn she is so beautiful.

    "Kallie, I hope you don't take this the wrong way, but I am

horny and it gets intense when I am ovulating. I'm not trying to have your baby but I am about to break my own rules with you," she confessed, as she made her way to me. "I have already broken many rules with you and I don't mind breaking many more," she added. "Kiss me Kallie." I pulled her to sit on me and didn't care if she felt my erection.

Before I could reach for her, she reached her hands behind my head and pulled me closer as she touched her lips to mine. It started slow and then it became fast and hungry. I have never been this turned on by a kiss like this before. She is a great kisser. My dick was ready for third base but my head was still in control. I wanted her to lead the way because I'm a gentleman. "Kallie, you kiss as good as you look," she said and then got up. Is that it? I asked a little frustrated, "Yes, that's it for me." She responded and winked at me.

ONYECHE

I have been very reluctant in opening up to another man until Kallie. I remember how badly I was mocked and laughed at when the news of my divorce was shared among family members and friends. Most of them stopped talking to me and others spread the news on social media, whilst laughing at me, behind my back. I was in such a vulnerable situation that I didn't get mad at what they were all doing. I was completely numb from the whole situation to the extent that it didn't bother me as much as others thought it should've.

I could remember feeling like there was someone else in me observing all that was happening on the outside. This happened when I stopped praying that God would change my husband and heal our marriage. I remember going to the church to pray. I walked around the church building, hoping that somehow God would change my ex and make our lives better. That didn't help the situation at all. While in the midst of that struggle, I came to a realization that if things were going to change, they would have changed already, from how much I prayed.. When I noticed that my prayer was becoming more like a pain than a healing, I changed the way I prayed. I started asking God to do what was best for me.

At that time, I was sick and tired of being sad and was ready to let go of all that was stealing my peace and joy. The moment I made up my mind to let go, was the moment the pain and suffering seized.

I became more hopeful for what the future held and I started doing things intentionally that made me happy. I noticed that the more I did what made me happy, the more it upset those who expected me to be sad. I had previously had many bad luck in my business but not anymore. Many opportunities I had been wanting opened up for me shortly after the chaos. It was as if the walls that imprisoned me suddenly came crashing down. I used to tolerate negative energy around me, but not anymore. I am so full of vitality and a new zest for life to the extent that I can't help but smile at myself now.
Kissing Kallie felt really good. Thank God I still have self control because I would've made love to him on that couch if I didn't.

Prior to kissing Kallie, I had not had intimacy with anyone for a long time. I have been cleansing myself in meditation and going out for walks in nature everyday. I had spent a lot of time healing and cleansing myself from the old energy which attracted the wrong people into my life. Kallie is a complete 360 turn around from the type of men I attracted in the past. He is nothing like my past and his dating history, from the little I have read about him is an enigma. There's not much known about his dating life because he values his privacy. He doesn't care about publicity but commands it. He is more interested in his game and charity organizations than his fame. He seems genuinely interested in me and really likes my kids too. It warms my heart to see him be so nice to my kids. My kids hardly like people but they seem not to have a problem with Kallie.

Oh boy but we only just met, yet it seems as though we have known each other for a long time. Where is this going? What would the media make out of this? I really do not care. Kallie is obviously in the middle of an important NFL season in which he needs to perform well for his team, if he wishes to have his contract extended. Yes, I read some press releases last night about the pressure on him to win this season. I want whatever we have or are building to be great and not stressful. The last thing I need is stress and I'm sure he feels the same way. Stress and I don't do well together because I like being happy and clear headed. The NFL may be tough but I believe Kallie can make his season what he wants to make it. Maybe I could just remind him that he already has everything it takes to be a champion and all he has to do is let that come out of him. I love football and my home team is really good and we could use a player like Kallie but I don't want to be selfish either.

He has all the ingredients that a champion is made of. I am now a fan and really want him to exceed his own expectations this season. Beith with him for this short amount of time, so far I have experienced a lot of firsts. No man has ever expressed their love for me like this barely twenty four hours of knowing each other and no man has shown this type of interest in my children's needs like he has. Obviously, he likes me or maybe he is going through an emotional shift. Either way, I intend to see where it leads before we part ways.

The kids took a two hour nap at Kallie's suite while Kallie and I spent most of the time talking. When the kids got up, we left for our room to allow him the privacy to take care of some team business.

KALLIE

Hello Coach Wells. Yes, I still have your SUV. When do you want me to drop it off and pick up my car? Okay. I'll be there. Bye. I have just spoken with Coach Wells on the phone. I guess it is about time I returned his SUV. I wonder if Onyeche and the kids need something from the store before I return Coach's car. I picked up my phone and dialed Onyeche's number. Oh, it says busy. She must be busy with her phone. I wonder who she is speaking with. Kissing her earlier was amazing and her lips against mine were really hot. I wonder if she'd like to do it again. Her boldness turned me on but I am a man of self control.

Part of being a man means knowing when to stop and following your girl's lead, never forcing anything. I wonder what she thinks now that I have expressed how I feel in just a short time of meeting. "Yeah, that was pretty weird Kallie," said his inner voice. "You just had to let it all out like that. Didn't you? Were you thinking straight or was it the pressure of the season that made you do that?" Asked his inner voice. I will take my chances. It was new for me and I don't regret expressing my feelings to her. If she ends up rejecting me, at least I will leave knowing that I let her know how I truly felt about her.

It is crazy how one minute I am thinking about how having a wife and kids would really feel like, only to have an experience that almost seems real. Hanging out with Onyeche and her kids makes me feel like they are my family. I find myself wanting to protect her and the kids. It is almost like my mind is on a speed dial to make things work for all of us.

Oh wait, I see her calling me.

Hey, I was just trying to call you. "Hey Kallie, yes I saw your missed call while I was on the phone with a friend," she answered. Okay, that's alright. I was just calling to ask if you and the kids need anything as I will be heading out soon to drop off the SUV. "Aww Kallie… That was very kind of you to ask but the kids and I have more than enough of everything for now. Remember you made sure of that earlier," she said. Okay. I thought I should ask. Don't make any plans for dinner because I'll be visiting and we will be ordering room service later. Oops! I am sorry if that came off as rude. I didn't mean it like it sounded. "Haha Kallie. You don't have to apologize.

We would love to order room service with you and you are welcome to our room anytime," she said. Okie dokie. I should be back by five thirty pm. Would that be good or is it too late for dinner? "Five thirty is perfect. I'll let the kids know you are coming for dinner and we will be ordering some room service," she responded. Sounds great. I'll see you and the kids later. When the call ended, I couldn't help but think about the changes I knew for sure were coming and I was looking forward to them.

My dad is my hero in every way. I respect how he takes care of my mom, me and my siblings. My dad was always there for us growing up. There was never a time when he was not present with us. He treats my mom with such great admiration and respect. To this day, in their fifty plus years of marriage, he still treats my mom like the most important person in the room and I love that about him. He always instilled in me and my brothers to respect women and make sure we find someone that we couldn't stop thinking about when they were not around because that is how to know you have found the one.

My dad always reminds us that a great society is made up of families with great values and he also made sure to remind us that kids are our future and should be treated with love, care and respect.

I have great respect for my dad and wonder how he would feel if I told him that I am involved with a single mom? What's important now is defining my relationship with Onyeche and everything else will have to wait. Who knows what the media have already posted after that incident at the zoo earlier? Whatever they may have posted really doesn't matter to me. I won't allow negative energy to come into what I am building with Onyeche.
I don't know why I feel this strongly about a total stranger in such a short time. Damn I feel a little bit uneasy about this whole situation but I still want to pursue it.
I better head to coach Wells because who knows what that old Bull has done to my car.

While I was on my way to see coach Wells, I couldn't help thinking about how my relationship with him and everyone else will change when I finally get married and have kids. I have heard from my other teammates with wives and kids that having a family changes you. Life is sweeter if you and your wife are crazy about eachother. They have often emphasized the point that it is important to marry a supportive wife.
Hey coach, I said as I stepped out of his SUV. "Hey Kallie. Hope you didn't drive my SUV too roughly? Asked coach. No, I didn't. I was more worried about you crashing my car. You know my car is a beast. "I did go for a fast spin in your car but didn't crash it, thankfully," he said. "Are you okay Kallie? Did anything crazy happen earlier today?" Why is coach Wells asking these questions? Did he read something?

No, everything is fine, coach. "Well, I read on social media that you were at the zoo with a gorgeous black woman and two kids. They said something like you all looked like a family. They could almost swear that the kids were yours because there was some sort of resemblance there," he explained. Hahaha really? I laughed because I couldn't believe what coach Wells was saying. "I know you don't like to talk to the media but this one is going viral fast. There was even a picture of the four of you trending." What? I have to warn Onyeche about it before it takes her unawares. "Who is Onyisi?" Asked Coach Wells. It's Onyeche and she is my friend. "Okay. How come I never heard about her until today?" He asked. Because I keep my personal business personal. "Oh like you kept the secret with what's her name? I think it's Jessica, the one that got paid by the media to share those romantic date pictures she took with you.

Might I add that she gained almost a million followers overnight after that?" Damn man. Well, thanks for bringing that up. To answer your question, this is different. Onyeche is not like Jessica and I am very excited about her. Anyways, coach, I have to go now. Enough talk about my personal life. I'll catch up with you soon okay? I quickly ended the conversation with my coach because I didn't want it to escalate and I also wanted to discuss some things with Onyeche.

ONYECHE

I am very happy that Kallie is coming over for dinner. It will be fun because the kids have never ordered room service before. I can't wait to see their reaction. My sisters are blowing up my phone on a family conference message channel. Apparently they have seen some social media posts about me. Why are you guys blowing up my phone? I texted. "Girl, we didn't know that you left your husband so you could go after a celebrity," Kia responded. What are you talking about Kia? "Well, let me say it again. You were photographed with Kallie, I mean the sexy ass Kallie himself at a zoo somewhere," she explained. Where did you get that from? I asked even though I already knew the answer. "Girl, I pictured you with all kinds of people but Kallie was never one of them. I mean, Kallie should go for a single hot mama jamma like me and not a single mom of two," she said.

What do you mean by that Kia? So you think men like Kallie shouldn't be attracted to me? "Yes, I mean no offense but you already have two kids and I have none. I am fresh and ready to mingle but you, you are kind of sour," she said disrespectfully. Well Kia, no wonder you are still single. Your attitude is what repels men from you. I am not sorry that Kallie finds me attractive and is interested in me. As per the media post, please don't send me messages if it is not an emergency because I don't waste my time on gossip. "Whatever, Onyeche. I hope Kallie realizes that he is making a mistake," she said before she stopped typing. I just ignored her. I could tell she was waiting for my response because she started typing but stopped. Kia has always been disrespectful and rude.

    I have to call Kallie and let him know about what I just found out. I know he doesn't care much about the media except on game days when he has to give an interview but I have no idea how this is going to impact him. I looked at my watch and it was almost five thirty. Kallie should be here soon.

I heard a knock on the door. As I made my way to the door, I hoped it was Kallie because there was a lot I had to talk to him about.

Who is it? I asked. "It's Kallie, Onyeche. Please let me in," he said. Oh ok. When I opened the door, I couldn't think of what to say because of the sight that stood in front of me. Damn, he is fine. When he looked at me, I could just feel my knees melt at his gaze.

    Since the kids were preoccupied with Peppa pig's latest episode and so what I did next was unexpected. I took a step forward towards Kallie and asked if I could wrap my hands around his neck? He nodded in agreement wondering or expecting what I was about to do. I got on my tippy toes and stretched myself to his face and kissed him gently on the lips. It was a quick one but the passion was intense. When I noticed Kallie pulling me closer with his arms wrapped around my waist, I stopped the kiss and broke away. I reached for his hand and announced to the kids that he was there. The kids immediately took off and came running toward him. I had never seen the kids act this way towards anyone. So this was another first for me. I stepped out of the way to witness the scene.

    Oiza jumped into Kallie's arms. He picked him up, said "what's up buddy," with an adorable smile on his face and then placed him back down. Then he turned to Oremeyi and did the same thing but this time, he asked her how she was doing? "I'm doing good," she responded. As I watched them interact, I couldn't help but notice the resemblance among them. Why does it seem like Kallie is the father of my kids? There is this striking resemblance among them that is almost alarming. I mean, I know who the father of my kids is but why does it suddenly feel like Kallie is their daddy? "Wake up girl from your dream. What makes you think that Kallie wants to be a family with you?" A voice like Kia's said to me. I quickly shook it off and asked him if he was ready to order dinner. "Yes, I am very hungry," he said. Oiza, Oremeyi are you guys ready for room service? "Yes, please," they responded together. Do you know what you want? I asked Kallie.

"Yes, I do. I want some spaghetti and meatballs with marinara sauce and some bread sticks," he answered. Yum! I think I might order the same thing for myself. "Oh sounds great. What would the kids like? Let's order a side of mashed potatoes and chicken fingers for them. I said. "Okay, perfect. I'll dial the number," Kallie offered as he made his way to the phone.
After he'd finished placing the order, he asked if Oiza and Oremeyi would like to order dessert and they both nodded in agreement. They made their way to Kallie and said that they wanted chocolate cake and orange juice. After the call ended, they were so happy that they got to order their own dessert over the phone.

He asked them if he could go talk to mama now that they had ordered dinner and they said that he could. They went back to watching the TV and left me and Kallie on the little sofa beside the bed. "Have you been on social media in the last hour?" Kallie asked. No but I know what you are about to talk about. My sister Kia let me have it after seeing the post about us. "Your sister? What did she say to you?" Kallie asked. Nevermind 'cos I already took care of it. "Please tell me what she said because it apparently hurt your feelings," he insisted. Well, she said she couldn't imagine why sexy ass Kallie would go for a single mom instead of a fresh girl with a lot to offer. I smiled while I said it.

"That's mean. I am really sorry that she said that to you," he apologized. You don't have to apologize, Kallie. I know I'm an amazing catch and anyone would be happy to have me. It's just unfortunate that I allowed myself to accept trash into my life in the past. Well, apparently I have stepped up my game with you. How are you feeling about it? I saw that they think you are my kids' dad. Does that bother you any? "Hell no! I love that they think that. The kids looking like me is the best compliment I have received lately," he answered with enthusiasm. "What would your parents' say about all of this? Does it bother you that they may not like this? I asked, curious to hear what his response would be. "No, it doesn't bother me. I mean, they are my parents and I love them to death but I still have to make my own decisions at the end of the day. Besides, I am a grown ass man and regardless of what anyone may think, I make my own decisions," he concluded.

Kallie doesn't seem at all bothered about what is going on outside. He is aware of it all but he doesn't focus on it. I respect him and a man who doesn't care what others think about him and who loves hard is very sexy to me. I love that quality in a man and have always secretly desired such a companion. I love hard and don't allow external influences to come in the way of my love either and so I can relate to him. I have been desiring someone with similar quality and didn't really think I would meet one until now.

Going through all the mess that I have recently recovered from, I learned so much about life and myself that otherwise I would not have learned. Though being rejected and scorned by longtime friends and close family members can be hard, there is always something good to be harvested out of every bad situation. In my case, I learned that most people are looking for drama. When they finally get it, regardless of how close they might have been to you, they tend to take sides with others they think are winning. Now I know that they were never really close friends. I would never rat on someone. I remember the one time I did it, my heart hurt for a while. I tried to fix things and made a promise to myself that I would not hurt anyone again.

KALLIE

I have never been one to make impulsive decisions but with Onyeche, I find myself diving deep and enjoying it too. All I am thinking about is being a family and protecting her and the kids. There is something about them that makes me feel like I am finally at home. I feel my heart being drawn to them like this was Divinely planned all along. And I don't even go to church that much. It has only been a couple of days but I am already planning a future that includes all four of us and maybe a little addition in the future. What is going on with me? Whew! I have no idea but I am pulled in the direction of making us a family as soon as possible. Tomorrow is when I leave town to meet with the team in Baltimore. I have to talk to Onyeche about staying in touch.

Since I left her hotel room three hours ago, I have been thinking about us and what happens next. I'll ask her if she would like to talk some more when the kids are in bed. "Hey girl. Are you still up?" I texted. Five minutes later she responded "Yes, I am. These kids are still awake and I just want them to go to bed so I can have some alone time," she texted back. "They are probably not that tired yet. I would like to come talk to you about something," I texted back. "I thought we already talked. What do you want to talk about?" She texted back. "I'd like to talk about what happens after I leave town tomorrow," I texted back. "Oh ok.

Could you give me a few more minutes to get the kids in

bed?" She texted back. "Sure. Please text me when you are ready and I'll be there," I texted back and then set the phone aside.

Thirty minutes later, I heard my phone beep and was desperately hoping it was a text from Onyeche. "Hey buddy. I saw the picture of you and a fine lady on social media today. I can't wait to hear all about her from you." My dad has never texted me this late in my entire life before. "Hey Dad. First time texting me this late and it's over a picture you saw earlier? I'll call you tomorrow man. Good night." I replied back. I heard another beep thinking it was my dad but this time it was from Onyeche. "Sorry it took an hour but I am ready for you now. You can bring your fine self to my room now." Her response gave me goosebumps and I just got up and left the room to meet her.

"Hey handsome," she said, opening the door for me to come in. "Hey Gorgeous!" I replied. She is wearing a pink satin nightgown with a nice pink zebra print robe over it. She looked so beautiful and I wanted to pull her into my arms and make more babies with her but I am a grown man and I have self control. "So, what do you want to talk about?" She asked me. Well, I pulled her to me and tilted her chin with my right index finger to look into her eyes. I wanted to drink the sight of her tonight because it would be a couple of weeks before I saw her again. "Ok.

We need to stop this right now because I am ovulating and my libido is high right now. If you keep doing this sexy thing Kallie, I am going to lose my control and jump you and I don't want to do that So. Back off sexy," she said but as she was about to step back, I leaned in and gave her a kiss anyway. She is lingering on the kiss but I broke it so it wouldn't progress any further. "Wow! That was hot and thank you for not forcing things," she said. I would never force anything with you Onyeche. We have our whole lives to have sex and make more babies. I wanted to make plans to see you again soon but I also wanted to make my intentions clear to you first. Are you ready for a real man in your life?

"Yes, I am," she answered, "Are you open to the possibility of being married again?" "Absolutely. I want forever with the right man," she said honestly. Okay. I am very happy that you are ready and want to be married again because I am ready and it would be my honor to show you the kind of man I am and hopefully you will say yes when I ask you to marry me. "Hahaha Kallie, we just met and there is still a lot to learn about each other before we walk down the aisle. I have been married before Kallie, as you already know. Marriage is different from dating and you are an athlete- a superstar athlete. Are you sure that this- us, is what you really want?" Yes, I am very sure and I hope to show you just how sure I am.

The next couple of weeks, I will be on the road. We will be in Baltimore tomorrow and will be playing the Seagulls Friday Night. Next week, we will be in Denver to play the Mountain Lions. I would love to come spend time with you a day before training begins. Also, do you have TV service? I would love for you to watch my game. "Okay. Well, take the week you will be in Baltimore to really think things through, ok?" Okay, I will.

"You can come visit me," she said and continued. Hand me your phone. I just typed my address in your notes. Yes, I have TV service and will be watching your game and taking notes too," she said.

Perfect. I am glad that we are on the same page. One more thing, please don't pay attention to the media, okay? Don't give an interview to anyone about us. Keep what we have between us and let it be our thing. I am not asking you to deny or confirm anything, I just want you to not grant any type of interviews okay? "Okay. Wouldn't dream of it. Kallie, I have one more condition to place on what we have." Okay. What is that condition? "Don't have sex with anyone else or be involved with any other woman if you really want to explore things with me okay?"

Okay. I already made that decision and I'm glad you mentioned it too. As for you, the same rule applies. I want us to be open and honest with each other at all times. "Sounds like a promise. You know, I came here with the intention of having a good time with my kids away from home but didn't think I would be involved with the Almighty Kallie himself," she added, smiling. Well, things change and sorry but you are now involved with the Greek God himself haha. I can't believe I just said Greek God. It sounds so weird to be described with those terms. "The terms fit perfectly. You are gorgeous and strong," she complimented. Well in that case, I never thought that I would have the opportunity to be captivated by The Goddess herself. I am truly honored. "You're welcome. I will miss you already, Kallie. Will you eat breakfast with us before you leave tomorrow morning?" Yes. I wouldn't miss it for the world and I have to say goodbye to the kids.

"They will be very happy to see you tomorrow morning. I think we should go to bed now. You have a long day tomorrow and the kids and I still have a few more days here before we head back home." Please take care of yourself and the kids and call me anytime. I promise I will return your calls if I miss them. "Okay. You have my number as well. Call or text me when you miss me." I will. Can I kiss you now? "Sure, you can."

The kiss was sensual and promising. I wanted to leave the pressure of my lips on hers. I wanted to leave the print of my lips on hers for her to remember me by, until we meet at her house in a couple of weeks. "Good night Kallie. See you at breakfast," she said.

Good night Queen. I'll see you at breakfast. Walking to my room, I couldn't help but think about how my life was about to change for good.

ONYECHE

Talking to Kallie last night was great. I am looking forward to the next two weeks but first breakfast. Kids, are you ready for breakfast? "Yes, please." Let's go downstairs. Someone is at the door. Who is it? I asked. "It's me, Queen," answered Kallie. "Good morning handsome," I said, opening the door to the gorgeous sight before me. I swear Kallie is in a league of his own in terms of male presence and beauty.

This man is fine and his energy is great. I reached for him, wrapped my hands around his waist and leaned in for a kiss. He didn't hesitate to reciprocate. "Mama, you just kissed Kallie," said Oiza, smiling. Yes, I just did. "Hey buddy. Are you ready for breakfast?" Asked Kallie. "I am but next time, you need to ask my permission before kissing my mom in front of me," he warned.

"Okay sir. I'm sorry for not asking your permission first," Kallie apologized. Oh well, can we go now? I am famished and Oiza, you are not my dad okay? "I am your son, mama and I am a guy," he said. Who are you and how old are you again? I asked my son. My kids appear to be growing up so fast before my eyes and it is scary and exciting at the same time.

"Hey Princess? Did you have a goodnight?" Kallie walked up to Oremeyi while Oiza and I were resolving our differences. "Hey Kallie, yes I did. Did you sleep well too?" She replied. "I did, Princess." Can we go now? "Yes we can," they all responded together like they planned it.

After breakfast, we walked to the kids play area at the hotel because the kids wanted to play. Before they went off to play, Kallie said his goodbyes to them. "Oiza, I will be leaving today but will be back in a couple of weeks to see you all at home. Will you take care of your mom and sister for me?" He asked. "I always do and I promise I will," he promised.

"Princess, I will miss you. Is there anything special you want me to bring for you when I visit in a couple of weeks?" Asked Kallie. "I want a new truck and a sports car." Answered Oiza before Kallie could ask him. "I want a new unicorn toy and a new kitchen playset," answered Oremeyi. "Noted. I will make sure I bring those for you okay?" "Mama loves the latest Yukon Denali in black too. She has been talking about it but has not got it yet. That's what I think you should bring her," said Oiza. "Oh so mama loves the SUV that I borrowed from coach Wells huh?" Asked Kallie. "Yes, that's her dream car," said Oiza. As I approached the kids and Kallie, I could not help but overhear their conversation. Are you all talking about me again? "Yes mama. I was just telling Kallie that you would like to have a brand new Yukon Denali, the exact one that Kallie drove us in," he said innocently.

Oh baby, it is not Kallie's responsibility to get it for me. I will get it for myself. I turned to Kallie to set the record straight. I don't expect you to buy me a car. Please disregard what Oiza just said. "Is that really your dream car?" Asked Kallie. Yeah. I really like it and will get it for myself when the time is right. I didn't want to lie to him. "Okay. Thanks for letting me know," he responded. Do you have to leave right now? "Yes, I have to. Can I take a picture of all four of us before I leave?" He asked me. "Sure you can. Kids, get over here for a picture with Kallie. Please Oiza, make sure you keep your face normal. "Keep his face normal?" Kallie asked. Yes, Oiza has this thing where he makes goofy faces in our pictures. "Well, let him make goofy faces. I'll make them with him," said Kallie. Oh no!

I can't have two goofy faces in my picture. I protested. "Are you ready?" Asked Kallie. Yes, I am. He takes a nice picture of us with his iPhone. I swear we look like one big happy family. Pictures really can create an illusion. Can you send me this picture? "Yes, I can." He said. Watching Kallie hug my kids and then get up and hug me made my heart full with love. I don't believe he is faking his interest in us at all. I feel so hopeful at this moment and nothing can take that away from me. Right before Kallie left, I saw a little bit of tear forming at the edge of his eyes. I didn't say anything about it because some things are better left unspoken.

KALLIE

Leaving Onyeche and the kids stings harder than I thought it would. I wanted them to come with me but also understand that they have things that they planned to do. I have no idea if I will be able to hold out for up to two weeks before I see them again but I'll try. I used to have doubts about having a family and raising kids but not anymore. Right now, I see myself as a capable father material. If there's something I want more, it's to be a father to Oiza and Oremeyi like my father was to me and still is.

Onyeche doesn't strike me as a woman who needs a man to thrive but I want her in my life because she is the missing piece. Since I arrived in Baltimore five hours ago, my teammates have been asking questions about the article they saw trending on social media but I have been ignoring them. I have made it clear to them that I don't want to discuss my private life with them. But there was one person I couldn't ignore and that person is Radcliffe. Radcliffe and I have talked about family life and he has been a good confidante when I need him to be.

"Oh man, how are you feeling?

I saw that article about you and that gorgeous woman." He said. I am feeling good. "Is she your woman?" I am still working on it. It's crazy that the way I have always wanted to feel about "The one" is how I feel when I am around her. "I know how you feel. Do you feel like she should be right here with you?" He asked. Yes, it was hard saying goodbye to her and the kids. Isn't it crazy though? Bear in mind that we just met but she makes me feel like all I have been looking for is now mine. "That is how you know, man. Does she feel the same way?" I believe she does. She is careful because of her past experience, that is why we are committed to making things work one day and a time. "Okay. That's a good start.

You just make sure to do your part and everything should work out." Thanks man. "No problem. When you meet the right woman for you, you don't let go. You do everything you can to make it work." I really admire your relationship with your wife and kids. You inspire me man. "Thank you. I love my wife and kids, they are my world and right now, they are waiting for me at the hotel."

Oh man, I can't wait until my wife and kids are waiting for me at the hotel too.

"You are not far from that man. Wish you all the best."

Thank you.

It's really nice to have someone who chooses to understand your situation and not judge you for it.

I'm really grateful for Radcliffe's friendship. I remember how wild he used to be until he met his wife. Before him and I became teammates, I heard about how three girls stabbed one another over him. The rumor was that he had invited one of them over to his hotel after an away game. Little did he know that the other two had seen his schedule and made plans to surprise him at his hotel as well. Don't ask me how they found out about where the team was staying. To this day, that is the mystery of the whole situation. When he and I became friends, I asked him what he thought about the situation and he said he was a bad boy and a player at that time but apparently, the game played him.

He had no idea that the three of them would show up at his hotel the way they did. When they did, he told them he never made promises to any of them. Instead of taking it out on him, the ladies turned on one another. When the police came to the scene, Radcliffe had an epiphany. He made up his mind that he was done being a player and desperately needed a woman who would make him want to stay with her whenever he had to leave. Someone for whom leaving the bad boy life would be worth it. It was as if God heard his prayers. Barely twenty four hours later, he met his wife.

She was dropping off some personal items to her sister who worked at the hotel. On her way out, she sighted him at the lobby drinking alone. There was something about him that struck her. She'd never walked up to a random man in her life until that day. She said hey and the rest is history.
What a story! They have a lovely family and Radcliffe's game went to another level since he met his wife. He is more respected and has completely turned his life around. I am so proud of him. Watching him interact with his gorgeous wife and kids inspires me.

I heard my phone beep and I took a look., was about to ignore it when I saw the name. It was Onyeche checking on me. "Hey Kallie. Just wanted to make sure you made it to Baltimore okay. Thank you for showing us a great time in San Diego. The kids send their greetings too." Hey Goddess. I made it to Baltimore alright. I will call you in a couple of hours okay? Send my greetings to the kids. "You're welcome. I can't wait to show you a great time in Colorado Springs soon. Thanks for the reply. Now I feel better, hearing from you and I'll let kids know you said hi." I don't remember the last time a woman I was seeing ever cared to check on me like this. It seemed as though they were more interested in letting the world know that they had just had dinner with me than checking on me. Okay, I'll take that back.

There was this one girl who really cared for me but she was more interested in pleasing her family than opening up to having a real relationship. Her parents thought that being with an athlete is a waste of time and she would end up alone. She didn't care to listen to what I had to say before she broke things off. When things ended between us, I wasn't heartbroken. I guess it all turned out well. The last time I heard about her, she was married to her high school boyfriend and they already have a baby together. Apparently it all happened within a month of our breakup. The whole situation made me feel like she was already seeing him behind my back.

Oh well, that doesn't matter now. I wish her all the happiness in the world.

ONYECHE

I am very happy to know that Kallie is doing well. I was so concerned about him and had to text to make sure he was okay. I hope he doesn't think that I am desperate for a man because I am not. Although I can't deny the fact that I am developing feelings for him, faster than I thought and I can't seem to get him out of my head. I think it might be because of my ovulation. There's something about my ovulation that makes my libido explode but this is different. This is almost like I could hear my vagina saying "I want Kallie, I want Kallie." It's like a whole opera going on down there and I can't seem to understand it. I guess I need to go for a run. Running always seems to work for me. My workout was great, I feel great and the shower I took afterwards was very soothing.

It's been two hours and I am looking forward to Kallie's call. I am excited to hear his amazing voice over the phone again. I'll let the phone ring twice before I pick it up. I can't make him think that I have been waiting for his call. I'm so excited to hear all about his day and how his team is preparing for the Seagulls. I guess I'm just so excited to hear about how he is doing. The wait seems like it is taking forever. It's been three hours and still no call from Kallie. Maybe he is running late and will be calling in the next few minutes. While I waited for his call, my mind was beginning to come up with many reasons why he hadn't called yet. "Maybe he just realized that you are not his type. Maybe he wants a woman he can have fresh kids with. Maybe he's just not that into you. Maybe he made the same promise to another woman and chose her over you."

If he ends up not calling, I won't send him a message or call him. I'll just move on with my life. After all, I am a survivor and life goes on. For the record, I am an amazing woman and mother. The right man would find me amazing and love me as intensely as I want to be loved.

In the meantime, I decided to look at my social media page and I couldn't believe how many comments I had on the last picture I posted. I took a peek at my inbox and I had over five thousand message requests. It was insane to me. Most of the comments are from random people and a few from family members and old friends who ditched me after they had heard about my divorce. Apparently, they want me to hook them up with Kallie's single teammates or players from the NFL. They believe their soulmates are in the NFL and God has placed me in the position to be their destiny helper. After reading some of these messages, I logged off my page. A lot of people have too much time in their hands to be mean and I don't have the time for such stupidity. I know I will be deleting a lot of messages later but not now. I have worked too hard on myself to stand firm on my feet to allow a fling to cause me to lose control of my mind.
Moreover, I have two amazing kids to care for and I intend to do just that with or without a man.

I used to believe in fairy tales until my life hit rock bottom and it woke me up fast. Now I know my fairy tale is not going to come from someone but me. My life experience has just made me smarter and wiser. I always choose to be as happy in the moment like I would be if I were to have my fairytale ending. Things happen in life but it is how you respond to each one of them that determines what you get out of life. Knowing all this, I think that I may have gotten my hopes too high with Kallie. I don't feel bad for how hot he made me feel and I won't get stuck feeling like the reason why he didn't call is because I didn't meet his expectations. I know that there's nothing wrong with me. Damn, I have never met someone who turned me on like he did.

    The kids have a new computer game that they have been playing for a couple of hours now and apparently the game is so amazing that they are completely carried away by it and haven't had to come hunt me down for some snacks. It's almost like I'm being avoided by everyone. Since I have all this free time, I guess I might as well watch a movie. My favorite movie of all time is "The Proposal," starring Sandra Bullock. I love how what initially started out as a fake engagement turned out to be something more. I could probably say the lines by heart but still I watch it to the end every single time. As I was getting ready to make myself a bowl of popcorn, the kids came running into the living room asking for dinner. Thank goodness I already set their plates at the table with their food ready to go. I like to plan ahead because I hate having to get up when I am in the middle of doing something important to feed them. So, I have learned to plan ahead in such a way that even if I get up to meet their needs, it doesn't affect whatever I am doing.

KALLIE

I just had my phone in my hands and suddenly it disappeared. Where could my phone be? I remember speaking with coach Wells about the new strategy we have planned for the Seagulls while I was trying to text Onyeche that I would be calling her soon. I remember Rico asking to borrow my phone so he could call his phone because he had misplaced it in the locker room somehow. I also remember holding off texting Onyeche so I could let Rico use my phone. I didn't want coach Wells to feel like I am not ready for this big game with the Seagulls because I have never been more ready to kick a team's ass for sleeping on me at the draft. I just wanted to make sure I let Onyeche know ahead of time that I would be calling her shortly or a little later depending on how fast Coach Wells finishes his lecture. I actually need my phone in order to be able to do that.

Coach Wells lecture took about one hour longer than expected and Rico left before I could get my phone from him. I wish I had memorized Onyeche's number. This whole thing is so stupid and I can't believe I let Rico take my phone. Thankfully, I know Onyeche's social media handle. I will message her on Instagram and hope that she reads her Direct Messages. I got on my windows surface pro and logged into my Instagram to message her and my page was blowing up. So many new messages and some strange comments from some strange woman asking me to introduce her to Rico. She said something about being Onyeche's best friend. Wow! She and Rico may really deserve each other. As I searched for her page, I secretly prayed that it was set to public because I needed to reach her. Thankfully her Instagram was set to public. I quickly sent her a direct message asking her to respond back with her phone number because I didn't have my phone with me.

    Her DM showed that she had just been on Instagram an hour earlier. I was desperately hoping that she would respond but I didn't get any response back after waiting a few minutes. Rico ended up returning my phone the next day after practice and I felt like killing the dude.

    He said he had left my phone in the locker and took his own but didn't realize it was mine he'd taken until he got home. This whole situation is just as if something is determined to make me look like a phony to Onyeche and that sucks.

    As soon as I got my phone back, I tried calling Onyeche. I called like ten times in a row but she did not pick up the phone. I followed each call with a text but still did not get a response back. This is really weird because she never takes this long to respond to my messages or calls.

I guess I deserve it because after all, I didn't keep my word last night. Even though it was not entirely my fault, how is she to know that? This sucks because I am an athlete and athletes already have a bad reputation of not following through after meeting a woman. I don't want the only woman who gives me goosebumps and the hope of having a family to think I'm a liar.I don't want her to break things off before I even get a chance to explain what happened. I don't know what to do right now.

    I wish I could go see her in person and apologize but can't do that either because of this big game tomorrow. How am I supposed to focus on this game when the woman I love is not talking to me? For all I know, she might have just shaken me off like I never happened and that would suck. There has to be a way to get in touch with her or I'll just show up at her place after the game tomorrow night.

    I just know that I can't let her write me off before we even get a chance to see what we could be. Damn if only Rico had not taken my phone with him. I honestly hope to God that she has not changed her mind about us. I love this girl and must show her through my actions. Why am I going out of breath just thinking about her and the possibility that she might have moved on already?

"Yo, Rico I'm not happy with you right now man. Your action might have just ruined something important to me," I texted Rico. "Oh man. I am sorry. I didn't do it on purpose. I hope that nothing is ruined for you because of me. You truly deserve the best." He texted back.

I hope your wishes come true Rico. I didn't text him back but silently hoped his wishes for me would come true.

  In the meantime, I decided to quit calling or texting Onyeche for now. I have already messaged her enough. If she still cares for me, she might text me back at some point but if she doesn't, I will show up at her door tomorrow night. She is not going to get rid of me that easily.Thankfully Colorado Springs is two hours behind Baltimore.

  I made some calls to a number of toy stores and the dealerships I could reach in Colorado. I had to make sure at least one of them had a brand new Yukon Denali that is black inside and outside and also fully loaded. I didn't want to spare any expense when it comes to my lady. I hope that my gestures don't seem too desperate. I might as well do what I already planned on doing anyways.

  Right before I went to bed, I texted her goodnight and asked her to say goodnight to the kids for me. I didn't mention my intentions because I didn't want to ruin the surprise I had planned.

ONYECHE

I have been ignoring Kallie's messages on purpose because I think I made up my mind to let go of him. I think everything we had was too fast anyways and I don't want to give too much attention to something that may end up being a waste of my time. I know he will get the memo eventually and quit disturbing me. Thank goodness the kids have not asked about him which makes it all even better. I don't want to bring my kids into an unstable situation at all. I may have broken my rule with Kallie when I let him get close to the kids but now that I'm moving on from him, I know my kids will be fine too. Afterall, they have a strong, independent mom.

After my ex father in-law took back his house, he had expected me and my kids to be homeless but they didn't know that one of my neighbors who was childless had left me one of his houses after he passed. I am still surprised at the timing of the event.

When the lawyers called me that he had left me a five acre property with a five bedroom ranch style home on it, I couldn't believe it. I had to ask them many times if they meant it or if I was being punked. They showed me the will and the details with my name on it.

My neighbor had been struggling to walk and needed help getting groceries and I remember telling him not to worry about his groceries because I would take care of them for him. I made sure he had groceries for almost two years and always looked forward to dropping them off. We had some wonderful conversations too and he often flirted with me and said if he was younger he would have married me. I always laughed and thanked him for the complement. He loved my kids and often made sure they had at least a new toy each month. It's crazy that he didn't have family to look after him. I was really happy to have been there for him for all that time. My ex used to accuse me of cheating with my 78 year old neighbor when we were together.

Although it hurt that he would accuse me of things that he was guilty of, I didn't let it bother me that much. When the lawyers handed me keys and paperwork to a fully paid home in Colorado Springs, I was so filled with joy. It couldn't have come at a better time.

My house is a little over 5,000 sq foot. My children have a ton of space to run around and I have a ton of space to do my work and also entertain guests.
The kitchen is open and connects to the living room. The house is brand new and almost the perfect picture of my dream home. I remember having some intimate conversations with my neighbor before he passed. I had told him what my dream house would look like and right now, being in this house is nothing short of a miracle because it is almost exactly like my dream house but better. In addition to the house that I inherited, Mr Richard had also set up utility accounts with at least $10,000 in each one for me. He had another account set up at the local grocery store for food to be delivered at the end of each week at the house. You could imagine how fast my life changed when only a few weeks before, I was worried about where I would live with my kids. I am more grateful for my life now, than I have ever been because what was supposed to tame me out, turned out to be a blessing in disguise.

Kallie not calling after he promised that he would hurt me but not that much. I am not stupid to think that a superstar athlete like him would completely keep his promise. I did hope for a second that all he was telling me was true but I am not a spring chicken anymore. I have to let him go. I have experienced too much pain to let myself worry about something that may not be for me. The good thing about my life now is that I realize that my happiness is not dependent on someone else but me. I choose not to get hung up on rejection. After all, it is always my choice the meaning I give to my experience. Even Kallie's sexy self won't make me back down from the decision I made to never let myself be broken or bitter again.

    I spent the whole afternoon baking for my neighbors. I have developed a love for baking and offered to make samples for my neighbors should someone need my services. This is one of many side interests that I enjoy. When I was about to complete cleaning up my amazing kitchen after hours baking, I heard a knock at the front door. I didn't remember leaving my gate open, nor was I expecting a visitor. Who could be at my door this late in the evening? I took a look at the clock and it was 9:45pm. Thank goodness Oiza and Oremeyi were already asleep upstairs. I turned on the front camera to see who it was. To my surprise, I saw Kallie standing outside my door. His eyes looked hallowed like he hadn't slept in a few days.

    Why was he here? Didn't he get the clue from my ignoring his messages? I opened the door, standing right in the middle with both hands blocking the doorway.

    Yes, how can I help you?

    "Hi Onyeche. Happy to see me?" He asked. In my mind, I wanted to jump into his arms and feel his heartbeat and have him wrap his muscular arms around me but the stubborn Queen in me had to put up a fight first.

    "Why should I be happy to see you?" I asked, pretending I didn't care.

    "Okay, I deserve that. I am sorry about not calling. I swear I tried to reach you as soon as Coach Wells released me from reviewing game film. I even messaged you on Instagram but didn't get a response from you. I swear to God, I didn't do it on purpose. I know it's what you might have expected since I'm an athlete but I promise you, I tried to reach you," he explained.

    "Okay, I believe you," I said and then reached for him by

his collar and pulled his lips to mine. The kiss was intense and my vagina woke up again. I turned to Kallie and said: "You have a spell on me. I don't know what it is about you but you make me melt." He smiled and said:

"Well, I hope it's a good thing."

Well, you are still here aren't you? And after that hot makeout session, I guess it's a good thing.

"I flew out here as soon as I could and I barely had any time to eat dinner because I wanted to make things right with you. Do you have anything to eat?" He asked.

Yes, you are in luck. I just made a fresh pot of fried rice and some chicken parmesan. Do you like chicken parmesan?

"I could eat just about anything right now," he answered.

Alright sir, come into the kitchen, let me feed you. walking into the kitchen, I could tell that Kallie was looking around and also staring at my butt. I turned around to look him in the eyes and then turned my back to him and rolled my waist. That made him laugh. "You are a sexy woman," he said. Thank you and you are a sexy man. You may have a seat. What would you like to drink?

"Water would be fine," he answered.

Coming right up sir.

I brought out one of my special dishes that I rarely use and made him a plate of rice and two large pieces of chicken.

"This looks and smells delicious. Thank you babe," he said.

You're welcome. I hope you like it.

I watched him eat his meal so fast and it was fun to watch.

"Where are the kids?" He finally asked.

They are in bed.

"Sorry I didn't ask about them earlier. I was so worried that you had given up on me before I even had the chance to make you mine officially," he explained.

Well, I almost did and that was because I don't want to be someone's last choice or side piece. I am too amazing to let myself cling or worry about someone who doesn't see my worth.

"I'm so sorry if you felt like I didn't see your worth, I didn't mean to make you feel that way at all. I had many things go wrong that night but the one that hurt me the most was thinking about what my not calling would have done to you," said Kallie.

Let's move on from that. You are here now and I forgive you. Moreover, it was not your fault and I am sorry for overreacting the way I did.

"So, you have a very nice house here," he complimented.

Thank you. I love it. It is truly amazing.

"I have a surprise for the kids when they get up in the morning," he announced.

You know you didn't have to get them anything right?

"Yes, but I did anyway. I love spoiling them," he added.

What did you get?

"I won't let you spoil their surprise. Can you wait till they get up tomorrow to find out?"

Hmm I don't know if I can. I'll just wait for you to go to sleep tonight and then I'll sneak out and go snoop around.

"No, don't do that because you will ruin your own surprise too," he warned.

You have a surprise for me too? You didn't have to get me anything. Aww Kallie. "You deserve the world my queen and I intend to spoil you with gifts. Speaking of tonight, would you mind if I spent the night here with you? I was in such a rush to get to the airport that I didn't make a hotel reservation." Of course Kallie. You can spend the night here. I have more than enough room for you. You can spend the night here on one condition though.

"What is the condition?" You and I spend the night wrapped up in each other's arms in one of the guest rooms.

"Oh yeah. I think I'll like that a lot. First, I need a shower and a change of clothes. Can you show me to your bathroom?"

Sure. It's that way to the left. It is connected to the guest room on the corner. "Okay, thanks. I'll need a towel and some soap too.

"I got you covered boy. It is all in the linen closet. Don't worry, everything is labelled in there.

"Okay. Thank you babe. You are amazing. One more thing, would you like to get in the shower with me?"

Nope! Tempting offer though.

My answer defeated my body's longing but I didn't care.

"Alright, I'll be a second okay?"

Okay. You'll find a white t-shirt and a pair of shorts in the closet. I left those in there in case I ever had a man stay the night. I said that to hear his response.

"What? Do you have other men apart from me? I am so hurt." He said, holding his chest playfully.

No, I was actually hoping you would come by and I bought these from amazon and placed them in there wishing that you would show up and now here you are.

"Wow, that's great to know. I'll see you in a little bit," he said and then walked into the bathroom and closed the door behind him.

KALLIE

I am so happy that she didn't kick me off her porch. Onyeche has a fire to her that I love. I was praying on the way from the airport to her place, that she would not allow her pride to get in the way of us and thankfully she did not. I feel so at home with her and I had no idea she knew how to cook. Dinner was amazing and now I'm taking a shower in her bathroom. This is all so new and amazing to me. Would she be happy with her present? What would she think of me when she sees what I got her? I hope she is happy with it and accepts it. I truly want to give her the world because she is fast becoming my world.

I was supposed to visit in a couple of weeks, yet here I am barely three days after we last saw each other.

"Kallie, are you doing okay in there?" She called.

Yes, babe. I am doing fine. Want to come in and help dry my body? I teased.

"No, tempting but no," she answered.

I will be out shortly.

"Okay. I wanted to give you a little tour of my space before we turn in for the night," she said.

Okay, just give me a second and I'll be right out with you.

About fifteen minutes later, I was finally ready to get a tour of Onyeche's grounds.

I like your mantel and the fireplace, they are amazing.

"Well, thank you. It's really nice," she answered.

You have a nice style girl and I feel so at home at your

place.

"That's great. I'm glad you feel at home at my place because this may just become your home too," she said, smiling.

I love how huge your kitchen island is. I mean look at all these pastries you have lined up on it and yet you have so much room for more stuff.

"Yes, I love it too and am glad I have this much space, else where would I place all these baked goods orders?" she responded.

Your orders? You run a pastry business?

"Well, kind of. I have just started trying it out and so I told my neighbors about it, not really thinking anything of it, but apparently, they are excited. Hence, all of these orders."

That's great. They will love your cooking because I sure did.

"You haven't even tasted my pies and cakes yet," she answered.

Okay, I'll try them right now but I have to tell you, from the food you fed me tonight, I have no doubt it will be amazing.

"Here, try this slice of my apple pie," she said, offering me a plate with a slice of apple pie that smelled delicious.

Mmm, delicious girl. See, I said it. You are the real deal. You're sexy, kind, compassionate, a great mom and a pretty amazing cook too. I struck a big one with you, girl. I expressed myself pulling her close to me for a kiss.

"You taste like my apple pie and I love it," she said.

Your pie is the best I have eaten in a while. My mom is an amazing cook and I used to think I may never find a woman who can cook as well as my mom but here you are. You are every bit as good a cook as my mom.

"What? Kallie, already comparing me to your mom? I don't know if I should feel good or bad about this."

You should feel good because I have never mentioned my mom's cooking to any woman before nor compared her cooking to anyone either.

You are fast taking over my heart girl and I don't know

what to do about it.

"Firstly, you are here; that means you did something about it. Secondly, you just shared your mom's compliment with me; which is great and finally, I forgive you for not calling me when you said you would."

What? I thought you already forgave me before feeding me. Hahah. Well, I'm glad that I am forgiven. Hey babe, as much as I want to tour the rest of the property, I am tired and would love to go lay down now. Can we go say good night to the kids before we go lay down together?

"Yes, we can. But I have to warn you to be very quiet because they are sleeping." I promise to be quiet, my love. I just want to see them tonight before they wake up in the morning.

"Alright' let's go this way," she said, pointing in the opposite direction away from the guest room.

We walked into a large master suite with a California king size bed in which two adorable babies were sleeping.

Look at how peacefully they are sleeping.

"I know, right? I love watching them sleep peacefully because that means I get to have some free time without being yelled at all day," she answered. I reached for her then, pulled her into my arms, standing behind her as we watched the little ones sleep. Something about this moment made me want to capture it in my heart forever. This is my family and I want nothing more than this.

"Hey, are you crying?" She asked. I had no idea that this moment made me so emotional.

No, I don't know what you are talking about.

"A tear just fell on my shoulder, Kallie."

I still don't know what you are talking about.

I tried fruitlessly to pretend but she saw through me.

"It is okay to cry but I want to know if I did anything to make you cry."

No you didn't do anything to make me cry. I just feel so much love here with you and the kids that something in me wants to hurry up and make us a family..

"Kallie, you need some sleep. Can we go to bed now? Maybe when you wake up in the morning, you will have more clarity and we can continue this conversation," she said, pulling me out of the master suite.

Woman, I know exactly what I want and it's making you and the kids mine.

"We'll see. Can we go to bed now?"

Yes, we can. She led me down the hallway to a spacious guest room with a Queen bed in it. The sheets smelled fresh and the pillows were perfect. As soon as I lay down, the last thing I remember saying was goodnight babe.

ONYECHE

I can't believe he came here for me and the kids. I never thought that he would show up even after I ignored all of his messages. This is truly amazing because no man has ever sacrificed like this for me before. Here is a man who has a lot going for him. He could easily meet another gorgeous woman to spend his time with but he chose to come find me and my kids. I really commend him for that. Although I acted as if I didn't want to see him earlier but deep down I was happy he came.

Now he is lying next to me, loudly snoring like a freight train and I can't help but think about how precious this moment is.

He is so emotional when it comes to me and my kids. Earlier when we went to say goodnight to the kids, I knew it was his tear I felt on my shoulders but he didn't want to talk about it. He is very determined to take our relationship to another level but I still have some questions.

I love how he is snuggled up to me while he sleeps and I feel trapped in his arms but I don't mind it at all. These bear arms make me feel safer than I have felt in a long time. It feels good to not try too hard to win someone's love for once. I think I'll allow myself to enjoy this for as long as it lasts.

He said he brought me a present and I have no idea what it is but I am excited to find out in the morning. This man makes life adventurous and though I am a little nervous, I guess it's not a bad thing. I have read a few articles and stories about celebri-

ties and their dating life but never thought that I would date one. I better go to sleep because my day is starting early. I forgot to ask him what he would like to eat for breakfast but I have a feeling that he would love whatever I make because he has already expressed how much he loves my cooking.
You know things are heating up fast for a man when he starts comparing you to his mom. I can not lie to myself and say that I am not surprised by all of this but I feel good, in spite of it all.

    I've spent a lot of time alone to heal from my past. I didn't want my past to look anything like my future. That is why I make deliberate decisions to do things differently now. I used to have a fear of being by myself and so I always made sure I had people around me even if they were not good for me. All of the people I had surrounded myself with whom I had thought had my back, turned their backs as soon as trouble erupted in my life. A few of them told me to my face that God had deserted me because I was sinner. They said they didn't want to get contaminated by me in any way.

    Of course I was hurt and rightfully so but then came to a sudden realization that has since changed my life. Most of the people that deserted have had many bad experiences too but I never walked away or judged them. I was there for them when they needed someone to talk to and a shoulder to cry on. I was even there when they couldn't clean their houses or find their way after a break up. See, I was hoping that because of my history with them, I could count on them. I had expected them to be there for me too, like I was for them but I was wrong. Instead they all disappeared from the scene as fast as they could when my life took a downhill spiral. The people who came to my aid were people I didn't even know that well. For a while there, I wanted to hold grudges against the friends and family who had turned their backs on me but I couldn't do it. The weight of the grudge was too heavy for me to carry. At that point, I wanted to release all of the pain and anger that somehow kept me stuck in a dark place I didn't want to be in.

    I learned from a life coach that the best way to rise above

something is to release the weight of anger, resentment and unforgiveness. As much as holding on to these negative emotions was justifiable, releasing them and letting go was the best decision I ever made. My whole world changed and I no longer need to have people around me to feel loved. I now enjoy spending time by myself and it is amazing. I now also enjoy doing quiet meditations to gain clarity and control of my mind. The level of my peace has increased and I no longer feel anger towards those who hurt me. Time to embrace this new and exciting adventure with a special someone named Kallie. "Goodnight my love," I whispered in his ear.

KALLIE

I slept great last night and it was probably the best I have slept in a while. I remember going to sleep with my sexy woman in my arms. She felt so perfect in my arms and I didn't want to let go of her at all. I smell bacon and some fresh biscuits... Oh look! She left me a note.
"Hey sleepyhead, when you wake up, come to the kitchen for some breakfast. I hope you like what I make because I forgot to ask you what you'd like for breakfast before you passed out last night. Do you know that you snore like a freight train? P.S. I will keep the kids away from the guest room so you can rest. Love, Onyeche." Aww what a lovely woman. Whatever you make, would be absolutely amazing, girl.

I stepped into the bathroom, found a brand new brush and a tube of toothpaste waiting for me. I quickly brushed my teeth and made my way to the kitchen. I was so excited to see the kids.

"Hey Kallie!" Shouted Oiza. He ran into my arms as soon as he saw me walking in the hallway. "Wow! You're here in our house. That's so cool," he said.

Hey buddy. I am happy to see you. You were asleep when I got in last night. Did you have a good night?

"Yes. I did. Did you have a good night too?" He asked.

Yes, I sure did. Now, I am ready for your mom's amazing breakfast.

"Good morning Kallie," greeted Oremeyi.

"Breakfast is ready. Come eat."

Good Morning Princess. It's good to see you again. I reached for her, gave her a hug and then put her back down to continue eating her bacon.

"Oh hey! Look who is awake. Sleepy head, hope you like bacon, eggs, sausages, biscuits, grits and cold cereal," said Onyeche. She had made a whole buffet of meals for us. I could not believe how much food she had made for us. This woman is the best and I think I'm gonna marry her.

Woah! Look at all this food. It smells amazing here.

"I hope you have an appetite because I went all out, player." She said, winking.

I do now, looking at how much you have made. Thank you for everything, Queen. "You're welcome. Now sit down and eat," she ordered.

There's so much to eat here and it is refreshing. I loved how she organized the food on the table. There were sausage biscuits here, biscuits and jelly there and right next to that was bacon and more sausages. This amazing woman really went all out for me that morning and I can't wait to make her mine. Breakfast was amazing and I ate more than I thought I would and there were still leftovers for lunch.

When I looked out to the back porch, all I saw was land stretching over five acres through the woods. This property is amazing and very scenic. There were big trees and bushes all around the property.

Hey girl, are you ready for your present? I asked her, waiting to see her reaction.

"You know, you didn't need to bring me anything but since you asked. Hell yeah! What did you get me?" I reached into my pocket and handed her the key to a brand new Yukon Denali. I had asked the salesman at Denver Car dealership to make sure a golden colored bow wrapped the SUV and keys.

"What's this Kallie? Did you get me a car? Wait, this looks like the key to the latest GMC Yukon Denali; my dream car," she said with excitement.

Yes, it is indeed. I remember how your eyes brightened when we drove in my coach's SUV and how you explained the details in the car. I had never heard a woman explain the content and details of a car like you did that day and I also remember the kids letting me know that's your dream car too. I wanted to be a part of that dream so bad and that is why I bought it for you. While I was still speaking, she jumped into my arms and gave me a kiss.

"Thank you so much for this. You just keep surprising me with what you do and how you do them."

You are welcome. For you baby, I'll keep doing my best to show you how much you are worth to me. 'Cos you're simply priceless and I am excited to make you mine.

"Where did you park the car? I have to go see it now," she said, pulling me towards the front door.

While she was pulling me towards her four car garage to the side of the house, I couldn't help but feel a sensation of calmness like this was home for me, finally. Here's a woman who doesn't ask for much yet deserves more than I could ever dream of giving her. I've always wanted a relationship like my parents have. My mom and dad always have each other's back and they compliment each other so well. My dad once told me that he doesn't know what his life would be like or if he would still be living today, if it was not for the love that he and my mom share.

I think I am beginning to understand what my dad was talking about because I feel like I can never let go of this woman and she is fast becoming my world.

"What?! It is real. I finally have my own brand new GMC Yukon Denali. Thank you so much for this, Kallie. This is a whole new level right here, babe. Look at this beautiful golden bow and ribbon around it. You did this boy," she added.

Yes, I did and for a worthy Queen like you.

"Wow! You got mama her dream car. So cool," said the kids.

Yes, I did because mama deserves it and now she can give you rides in it too.

When I turned to look at Onyeche, she was embracing the steering wheel and dashboard like you would a newborn. It was such a beautiful sight to see for sure. I just love to see people's dreams come true and it is even better when I'm a part of it.

"Hey guys, wanna go for a ride in my new car?" She asked us.

Yeah!! The kids and I responded with excitement. I helped the kids into the SUV and slipped into the front seat with her afterwards.

"Alright mama, where are we going in your new whip?" I asked

"I'm gonna give you all a ride around the neighborhood. Kallie, are you ready to check out your new neighborhood in style?"

Hell yeah! "Let's go!"

While she drove us around the neighborhood, I felt my heart expanding with joy and happiness. I have found my family at last. I have found the one that makes my heart feel at home. I could feel the approval of a voice in my head or heart and it felt peaceful. As she drove us around the neighborhood, I couldn't help but notice that every neighbor had at least two acres of land around them and they all seemed to have horses and cows also but it didn't smell bad in the air.

I have been to small towns where there were horses and cows and the smell in the air was a little bit too hard to bear but not this one. I turned to Onyeche to ask how she was able to contact her neighbors about her business when the houses are not that close together.

"Well, I just went and knocked on each of their doors and asked if they would like to try my pastries. They were glad I stopped by and were happy to know that I live in the neighborhood. Some of them ordered right away even before trying it," she explained.

Wow! You are brave. You didn't think about rejection huh?

"No, I didn't think too much about rejection because I

have learned to focus on what I want and not what I do not want. Since learning this strategy, life has been better and more enjoyable. If I get rejected along the way of going after what I want, I just hold the thought that something better is coming."

You are one rare gem. Do you know that?

"Yes, I do and now you do too," she said, winking at me.

"Hey, what's on the back seat?" Asked Oiza. He just sighted the present I got for him and Oremeyi. Oh, it's something special for you and the Princess. You didn't think I forgot about you did you?

"Can we open it up now?" Princess asked anxiously.

No Princess, wait until Queen mama gets us home before you open it up. "Awww…Mama, can we go back home now?" Asked Oiza, he too was becoming anxious.

"I guess we can. I have enjoyed cruising in this new car. Thank you Kallie. You're the best," said Onyeche.

You are welcome. I am glad you like your new car.

ONYECHE

Driving around this neighborhood in my brand new car felt great. There's something about a brand new car that makes you feel good. So grateful that Kallie thought of me this way. It was a good surprise for sure. Now, I feel like taking a road trip in this beast.

"Don't open your presents just yet, guys. Wait until we get into the house," I said to the kids because they were becoming too anxious to open their presents. I parked my new car in front of my garage and stepped out to help the kids out. Kallie quickly went ahead of me to start getting the kids out. I swear I don't know what I did to deserve such a thoughtful man.

"Please, let me," said Kallie, when I tried to open the door into the house.

Kallie, you are one rare gem of a man and I could get used to this.

"Mama, can we open the presents now," asked Oiza when we finally got the presents in the house.

Yes, you can. Kallie, do you mind helping them open it?

"I would be happy to," he said.

"Oh wow! This is so cool," exclaimed Oiza. Kallie bought him an electric remote sports car. It was a battery-operated Batman car.

What do you say baby?

"Thank you Kallie for my new Batman car," said Oiza.

"You're welcome, buddy. I hope you like it," said Kallie.

"I love it," answered Oiza.

"Wow! Baby, this is a very nice car. It is almost like Kallie knew what you have been hounding me for," I said admiring the car.

"Wow! Mama, this unicorn is really nice too, mama" said Oremeyi when she was handed her own present.

Yes, baby it is. It is a unicorn cat just like the one you lost at church last month. I guess

God was looking out for you baby. Now you have the exact same toy you lost.

Thanks Kallie for making my baby smile.

"You are most welcome. I am happy to be a part of your excitement right now," he said. "Mama, Kallie is a miracle worker," said Oremeyi.

He sure is, baby. I looked at where Kallie was standing and he had a big smile on his face. I blew him a kiss and he caught it with both hands and placed it over his heart. It was the most adorable sight.

"I still have one more gift to give the kids. Everyone wait here, don't move. I'll be right back," he said and then walked out the front door.

A couple of minutes later I heard someone else's voice outside and it was one of my neighbors; Mr Dennis. He is a fan of the Pirates and couldn't contain himself when he spotted his favorite player. "Dear God, if it ain't Kallie. Is that you or do you just look like the superbowl contender, NFL star QB from the Pirates?" I overheard Mr Dennis ask Kallie. I ran to the door to eavesdrop on their conversation.

"Well, hello there. You know me so well. Nice to meet you," said Kallie offering a handshake.

"My name is Dennis and I'm the neighbor to the beautiful woman who owns this house," he answered. Of all the places I have dreamed of meeting you, I never thought you would come right to my doorstep. My God, ain't the good Lord great?! I watched the game last night and you, my boy, did your thing as always. I'm super proud of you son," said Mr Dennis.

I watched as Mr Dennis gave Kallie a hug and had tears of joy in his eyes. You could tell that Kallie's presence impacted him positively. Kallie hugged him back and said thank you.

"Thank you for the love and support, sir. It is truly appreciated," responded Kallie.

"So what are you doing at the pretty lady's house? Is she your gal?" Mr Dennis asked. "She is my lady Mr Dennis. I came by to spend some time with her and the kids before our next game in Denver." As soon as I heard Kallie's last response, I opened the door to see a very happy Mr Dennis.

"Hey Mr Dennis. I see you have met your favorite baller," I said with a smile.

"Oh Hello there, pretty lady," said Mr Dennis.

"I had no idea you knew Kallie personally because if I did, I'd have treated you better," said Mr Dennis. I smiled after that response because Mr. Dennis is one of the nicest people I have ever met

"Nice to meet you Mr Dennis. Hey, babe I'm headed to your car to pick up the remainder of the kids' presents," said Kallie.

Sounds great, babe. Turning to Mr Denniis, I asked; was there anything I could do for you today?

"Yes, milady. Do you have some of that amazing pecan pie of yours?" He asked.

Oh no, I'm sorry. I don't have any more left but I have a pan of my amazing apple pie left. Would you like to sample it?

"How much is it? I would love to pay you for it. I hate to have you take all this time to make it and don't get compensated for it. You are too good to bake for free," advised Mr Dennis.

Well, thank you for the encouragement Mr Dennis. If you would please come in, I'd be very happy to give you some apple pie.

"Okay, but first I need to ask your man's permission. Hey Kallie, is it okay if I went into your lady's kitchen?" He asked Kallie who was carrying two boxes into the house. "Yes, you can Mr Dennis, as long as you keep your hands off her you are safe," he answered, smiling.

I gave Mr Dennis the last pan of my apple pie and he was very happy with it. After he left, Kallie called the kids together and handed them the additional presents he got for them.

"Hey Princess, this one's for you," said Kallie.

"Wow! It is my new kitchen mama," said Oremeyi with excitement.

Yes, it is. It is much bigger than your old one and the pot collection is bigger as well. What do you say to Kallie?

"Thank you Kallie for my new kitchen set," she said.

"You are welcome. I'm glad you like it. Now you can learn how to cook like your mama," he added.

"Where is mine? Did you get me something else Kallie?" Asked Oiza.

"Of course I did. Here's your final present," said Kallie, handing him a nice Blue Chevy Silverado toy truck.

"Wow! It is very nice and I like it very much," said Oiza.

What do you say to Kallie, baby?

"Thank you Kallie for giving me my new truck," he thanked Kallie.

"You are welcome buddy," responded Kallie.

Kids, you can take your toys to your play area and play.

"Mama, can you please help me move my new kitchen to the playroom?"

Yes baby, I'm happy to help.

"Oh no, let me do it," offered Kallie.

The playroom is right past the laundry room to your right.

KALLIE

I have been having such a great time with Onyeche and the kids and it seems so amazing. The kids love their presents and mama loves her new car. I must say that I feel good being a part of their joys. Now it is time to talk about what's next with my woman. My next game will be in Denver and after that we go for a bi-week. Next week I will be off and be back the week after to play the Patriots. I know I can get a lot done in that one week that I will have off. I am also thinking about spending it with her and the kids at my parent's in Michigan. I want them to meet my folks.

Onyeche, can we talk for a bit?

"Yes, sure. Is everything okay babe?" She asked.

Yes, everything couldn't be more perfect. I wanted to talk about where we go from here and my upcoming schedule.

"Okay."

We play the Mountain Lions this Thursday in Denver and after that, I have a whole week of break before we play the Patriots; a very big rival.

"Okay, sounds like you guys have a big one ahead of you but I have no doubt that you will help your team win that one too," she answered.

Thanks for the confidence you have in me, babe.

"You're welcome."

So, I was thinking about reserving a special place for you and the kids in Denver for the game and driving back here afterwards. What do you think about that?

"You want us at the game in Denver?"

Yes, babe. It will mean the world to me to see you and the kids in the stands cheering for me.

"We wouldn't miss it for the world babe. I would love to come and watch you kick my home team's ass," she said, smiling

Haha… Okay that sounds great. I was also thinking that we could drive back here after dinner in Denver. Because I would like to spend a couple of days here with you and the kids and then take you to Minnesota to see my parents, sometime next week. What do you think about that?

"Wow! That's a big step Kallie. Are you sure you want us to meet your parents this early?"

Yes, it would mean a lot to me and I would love to meet your parents too.

"Can I think about it? Oiza has school and Oremeyi hasn't started school yet. I have to plan with Oiza's teachers to make sure they can accommodate his absence and he doesn't miss much at school," she said.

Sure, you can. Thank you so much for doing this for me, I really appreciate it.

"You are welcome Kallie. I am delighted to meet the people who raised you, babe," she added.

They will love you and the kids too, I promise.

"What time are you meeting the team in Denver tomorrow?" She asked.

I told them that I will be meeting them at 1:00 pm tomorrow. That would give me enough time to get ready for first practice before the game on Thursday.

"Okay, sounds great. How are you getting there?"

I was thinking about renting a car to Denver. I already made arrangements with the dealerships that I purchased your car from and they offered to pick me up tomorrow at 11:30 AM as a courtesy for supporting their business.

"Oh that's nice of them. I was going to offer to drive you because Denver is only 45 minutes away. It's not too late to cancel with them babe because I am more than happy to drive you to your hotel," she offered.

Babe, I don't want you to bother about it. Besides, I already spent a good deal of money at the dealership, so I might as well accept their bonus deal. Moreover, I would rather you take the time to prepare for the changes coming soon. Your life will be different babe, with me as your man. Are you ready for that?

"I am ready, I think," she answered.

Spending time with Onyeche and the kids the past day and a half has been amazing. This woman can cook and just knows exactly what it is I want. I couldn't let her go now. I think I am hooked and I like it.

"Hey man? Have you read what is being said about you on social media lately?" I got a text from my brother, Ian. Ian and I are very close and he is my best friend.

No man, you know I don't care about social media.

"I know you don't but I wanted to give you a heads up. They are saying something like the woman you are with is a gold digger trying to take your money from you," he texted.

Ian, they have the freedom to say what they want and I have the freedom not to pay attention to it.

"Okay man. I got your back. I'll try to make them take it down as soon as possible."

No man, don't bother. Just let them do what they want, it doesn't bother me at all. I'll see you at mom and dad's next week okay?

"Can't wait. Hey, kickass tomorrow okay? We will all be watching."

Sure thing and thanks. After Ian and I ended the conversation via text, I had to look for Onyeche to let her know what was being said just in case she might have seen it and was bothered by it. I found her cooking something delicious in the kitchen again.

Hey woman, you look sexy in that apron.

"Hey man, thank you."

So, I wanted to share something with you to make sure

you are okay.

"Okay. What is it you want to share?" She asked.

So, some malicious magazines and social media sites have started spreading fake rumors about you and me. I just want you to know that I don't pay attention to their crap and you shouldn't either okay? I want us to focus on each other and build what we have without paying attention to negative media.

"Oh trust me, I don't pay attention to that stuff. They are entitled to their opinion as I am to mine. Nothing anyone says or does will change how I have started to feel about us okay?" Okay, that makes me feel better.

ONYECHE

Kallie just left a little over an hour ago and I already miss him. He fits perfectly into our lives and it feels right with him. I cannot believe how much memories we are fast creating together and it is amazing. The kids and I will be there Thursday night to watch him play. Kallie advised me to go through the players entrance when we get to the Mountain Lions stadium and let them know that we are his family. He said he would give them a special question to ask me and that I already knew the answer to it. I have no idea why Kallie was messing with me like that but I am excited to watch him in two days.

  Hello Mrs Dale, it's Oiza's mom. We will be going out of town the whole of next week and I wanted to reach out and let you know about our plans. I'll be happy to come by and take Oiza's homework for the week we plan to be away.
I was just on the phone with Mrs Dale and she said Oiza is excused because he is one of her top students and she has no doubt he will be able to catch up with what they cover while he is away.
  Now that I have taken care of that, I need to make sure my business partners know that I will take that week off for important family business. Well, Kallie is now family whether I like to admit it or not.
It is finally Thursday and we are on our way to Denver. I left early so the kids and I could have lunch at Chick fil a and visit some friends before we head to the game. I sort of like road trips now, especially one taken in my brand new Yukon Denali. This car is

amazing and this is the longest journey I have taken in it since I was blessed with it. I have been complimented by at least five people at every stop we have made so far. This SUV is even better than I thought it would be.

After lunch at Chick fil a, we made a stop at Halima's place. Halima is one of my closest friends. She is one person I can confide in when I need someone to talk to. Halima is married to the president of a fortune 500 company in Denver and her life is busy. I rarely get to see her but when I do, we always have a great time. Halima is great to talk to but never available when you need material support.

I think it is funny that she has asked me for more stuff than I have ever asked her. Her husband is very wealthy and makes sure Halima and her kids are abundantly supplied but for some odd reason, Halima is always fascinated with my stuff. She never hesitates to ask me to lend her a piece of jewelry, a pair of shoes or even a dress I wear that she thinks looks good on me. She always likes my stuff and I find it hard to say no to her. I remember seeing a nice piece of jewelry on her recently. I asked her if I could borrow it. I was sort of joking with her because I never ask her for stuff. She said she couldn't give it to me because that was the only piece she had. She went on to explain that her husband bought it as a gift and would ask about it if she was not wearing it. I said it was okay if she didn't let me borrow it. That incident was not the first time I had tested her to see if she would reciprocate my generosity and as usual, she said no to me.

I love talking to her when I have the time. Lately, I am beginning to think that maybe I need better friends since the closest one I have is this selfish with her stuff yet always expects me to be generous with mine. When we stopped by her place, she ran outside to see us. Apparently she had noticed my new car from the window upstairs and ran down to see who it might be.

"Hey sis, what are you doing in a brand new Yukon Denali? This looks exactly like the one you have been talking about getting forever. I see you have finally done it," she said.

Hello Halima. It is nice to see you too. Hope you and your

family are doing great?

"Yes, we are fine. Pardon my rudeness sis. When did you buy a new car? Your monthly payment on this thing must be really high."

Sis, I didn't finance it, it's a gift from a friend. "Which friend? Last time I checked, you don't have any friends but me and I didn't buy you this car."

I met a nice man who got it for me.

"A man? Hmmm You are finally dating? That's amazing but a couple of weeks ago you didn't have anyone and now you do?" I nodded my head in response because I didn't want to explain further.

"Please spill the beans girl. I want to hear every little detail. Don't leave anything out okay?"

I don't want to say anymore about my relationship, Halima. Can we at least come in before you wear me out with your questions. See why I say you should've studied law?

"You know I'm going to find out one way or another right? Whoever this new man is, I hope he treats you well because you deserve it."

Thank you sis. I really appreciate that.

We spent the next 2 hours at Halima's. I think she spent most of it trying to get more information from me about Kallie but I made sure not to say anything about it.

We are headed to the Mountain Lions game, do you want to come? I offered out of courtesy but hoping she would say no.

"I would love to but my husband and I planned this special dinner for the family tonight. He even bought me a special dress for it too. I am super excited for it because I get to dress up and someone else is cooking."

Oooo sounds romantic. I think you guys are going to make another set of twins tonight. "Oh God, No. Thanks for the prayer but no. Ethan and Alan are already a handful as it is. I don't think I can handle more hyperactive, loud and crazy kids anymore."

Hahah… remember when you used to wish for ten children? What happened to your wish?

"Girl, I changed my wish since I had twin boys.

Life is plenty busy with them and I won't be able to handle anymore. You know, Brad would agree with you about making more babies. He would like a girl in the mix too."

Well, give him what he is asking for. I believe God will give you strength to handle them. "Says the mom of two. Why didn't you have more when you and 'you know who' were still together?"

Okay, I think I'll terminate this conversation. You have been amazing the last two hours girl but I think we better start heading to the game because it is 30 minutes to kickoff and it will take us 20 minutes to find parking.

"Alright sis, thank you for stopping by today. It was really nice to see you. Maybe

I'll come by sometime next week and see all the changes you have made to your new house. Girl, it seems like everytime I see you, something amazing is happening in your life. Who knows? Maybe the next time I see you, you might have a big rock on your finger and tell me you are engaged to a celebrity," she concluded.

Haha… you have an active imagination, Halima. Love you sis, I'll see you soon okay? "Bye kids and bye my friend."

I was so happy that Halima has a massive playroom for the kids. As soon as we got into her house, the kids ran to her playroom to be entertained. They were a little hesitant to leave but they said bye to Halima and walked out the door with me.

Hi, my name is Onyeche and these are my kids; Oiza and Oremeyi, we are here for Kallie. "Oh I see. Ma'am what is the name of your favorite car?" Asked the security at the players' entrance. Funny you asked but it is actually the one I currently drive. My favorite car is the GMC Yukon Denali. I love the black color and black leather interior, that thing is amazing. I started rambling about the car and remembered to stop when he handed me a note from Kallie and opened the gate for me to go through.

"Hey girl, I knew you would ramble about your new car. Welcome to the game and I will be looking out for you and the kids from the field okay?"

I smiled at the notes and headed to the third row from the players bench right behind the Quarterbacks chairs. Seemed like that row was reserved for family and friends. Barely 10 minutes after our arrival, a vendor with powerade, hotdogs and popcorn came over to us and placed a lot of food in front of us. I was quick to say we didn't order anything but he smiled and said it was all taken care of. Apparently, family and friends are entitled to be served refreshments during the game. The kids were super excited and immediately started eating their popcorn and drinking their powerade.

Kickoff started a little later than expected but it was worth it because as soon as Kallie and the rest of the players came out through the tunnel, he looked at where he'd expected us to be and winked at me. He was happy to see me and the kids and it felt good to have that connection and understanding with him.

KALLIE

I hope that Onyeche and the kids make it to my game on time. I am really looking forward to their presence. This anticipation feels so intense like this is my first ever professional game and my parents are finally here to witness my dream come true. Only in this case, I feel like this is my wife and children coming to watch daddy play the game he loves. That definitely feels great for real and we will be having dinner together and driving back to Colorado Springs tonight. I just hope that I could be interviewed first so I can get out early enough to catch my family. 'My family,' that definitely sounds great. Standing behind this tunnel is exciting not just because I am about to go play the game that I love but because I have three special people in the stands waiting to watch me play.

  As soon as we stepped out of the tunnel, I couldn't help but look up at the stands hoping to find my people. It turned out they were also looking for me. When I locked eyes with Onyeche, I winked at her. She was wearing a fitted t-shirt with my team colors and with my number on it. The kids were also wearing my team color to show me support. I didn't expect that. It was amazing to have her support me like that and she looked so sexy in that tight fitting shirt too.

  "I can't wait to give her a kiss after the game," I thought. I have never felt this grateful to see someone in the stands to watch me play. I mean, my parents and friends have been there many times to see me play in different cities but I have never had this type of feeling of joy from seeing someone I care about in the stands, like I do right now.

I had often imagined how happy I would be to look over at the stands and see my wife and kids cheering me on. The highest I have ever felt doesn't equal what I am feeling right now. Seeing her and the kids wearing t-shirts with my number on them while screaming my name, made me so proud.

We got the ball at the coin toss and we started the offense. My first pass was a 65 yards touchdown. It was quite the throw for me and I turned to see what Onyeche was doing and boy was she going crazy in the stands. I bet I could read her lips and could tell she was yelling out "that's my man," in the stands. You're damn right girl, I found myself responding back. The game was a blow out. We scored 38 straight points to Dnever's 3 points.

After the game ended, I ran up to the stands where my girl and the kids were and gave her a hug and a kiss. I whispered in her ears that she was my good luck charm tonight.

"Oh no, babe. You don't need a good luck charm, you are already so damn good," she responded back.

Thanks babe but I think your presence here made a difference to me. You don't know how many times I have looked in the stands visualizing my wife and kids watching me play, you being here, made it even better. "Aww...Kallie, that sounds so sweet. I'm happy to always be in the stands cheering you on boy because you deserve it," she answered.

Go up there to the family lounge and wait for me, okay? I am going to talk to the coach and the team, take a shower and maybe do a 5 minute interview and then I'll be back there to go to dinner okay?

"Okay, babe. The kids and I will be up there and there's no need to rush because we ate a lot of snacks during the game," she said.

Oh baby, I love how you always have the perfect response to my concerns. Hey kids, I will be back in a little bit okay? I love you guys so much.

"We love you too, Kallie and we are so proud of how you

played tonight," she said to me before I left for the locker room.

After I finished talking to her and the kids, I noticed that a reporter had a camera close by and may have taken a picture of me and Onyeche but at this point, I didn't care. Matter of fact, anyone can say what they want and it still wouldn't bother me. Making sure that Onyeche and the kids are safe and taken care of is my top priority right now.

Hey coach, I hope your talk is not for an hour tonight because I have got somewhere to go with my family.

"Hey superstar, that's fine. It'll be just five minutes. What happened out there tonight?" Asked coach Wells.

What do you mean man?

"I have never seen you play with so much finesse like you did tonight. I mean, you are a great player but tonight was a whole new level. Matter of fact, I was hoping we would win but I didn't expect a blowout," he explained.

I was ready to play tonight and plus I wanted you to have a shorter team talk tonight and in order for that to happen, I would have to win.

After our team meeting, I took a quick shower in the locker room and only had a 3 minutes interview with NBC Sports after which I said my goodbyes and went for my family. I found my girl and the babies sitting at the corner in the family room looking bored. Hey guys, hope I didn't keep you waiting too long?

"Kallie!" The kids called.

Hey kids, are you ready to go get dinner?

"Yes, we are." I turned to Onyeche and asked how she was doing before giving her another hug.

"I'm fine, I just need some food."

That's a good thing because I need some food too. I already made dinner reservations at the JW Marriott. I heard they serve amazing steaks and a large variety of options to pick from.

"That sounds amazing because they are only about fourteen minutes away," she answered. Let's go family because papa is famished after a 3 hour game.

"Alright papa, let's hurry and get you some dinner before you pass out," she said, smiling.

ONYECHE

This food is so good Kallie. I didn't think it would be this good. Who recommended this place?

"One of the Mountain Lions players; Payton. Him and I go way back in college. Payton was my running back in my freshman year of college at Michigan state. He was drafted in his third year and we didn't stay in touch until I got drafted four years later in my senior year. Payton said he brings his family here all the time for special occasions or whenever he could convince them to go to dinner for no reason," He answered.

Payton has very good taste then because this is very delicious.

Look, even the kids ate all their food without complaining. Whoever the chef is, I would love to get his number.

"Maybe he could cater our wedding. I bet everyone would go wild about the food at our wedding," said Kallie. I wasn't expecting Kallie to mention a wedding but he has a way of surprising me and I am still learning to get used to it.

Our wedding huh.

"Yes, our wedding," He answered as a matter of fact.

Kallie, you know you actually need a proposal before a wedding right?

"I'm working on it, babe. You will really like it too and won't hesitate in saying yes," he responded.

Wow! The confidence you have there.

We left the restaurant and started back for Colorado

Springs about an hour and 15 minutes after dinner. Kallie insisted on driving us back but I stood my ground and held on to the key.
"You have been busy all day and I haven't been as busy as you, so it is only right for me to drive us home. I need my man to rest after such an epic game tonight and not worry about driving us home," I responded clutching the keys.
"I'll let you drive us home this time because you are right. I have been busy all day and I am really tired after the game," he said, trying to convince himself to lay low.

Kallie, you are amazing and I am so happy to witness you have a career yard touchdown and a record breaking game tonight.

"Thank you, my lady," he responded.
We drove in silence for the next 30 minutes. I turned to look in Kallie's direction and he was knocked out. The kids were also knocked out. Apparently, they were very tired and couldn't wait to get to sleep. The sight of my sleeping people was so adorable and I couldn't help but enjoy this moment in silence.

A couple of years back, I didn't know this type of life was possible because I was so busy living my life trying to fix what was broken. In the process, it broke me or at least tried to break me too. How I made it through those tough years still baffles me but one thing is for sure, I have faith in God. No matter what the situation I face, I always cast the burden on Christ within me and go free. I don't deny the situation by any means but I always deny its power to affect me.

Coming to this place where I could deny the power of negative situations over me was not always easy but perseverance helped me get there.

While Kallie is talking about hiring a wedding caterer already, I'm over here enjoying each moment with him. Though he is already like a thousand steps ahead of me and it's not scary at all. How could a man this successful and sexy make such hasty decisions when he hasn't even met my crazy family yet.

He has just jumped in and is assuming the role of a father

without holding back. We have not even talked about where we would live but he has expressed his willingness to move to Colorado Springs if that is what it would take to have me in his life. This is my life now and it is almost too good to be true but I do believe miracles happen. It is often easier to believe in fairy tales for someone else but yourself. This does have parts of a fairy tale but so far, it has been unbelievable.

"We are home…" I announced as soon as I parked in the garage. They still didn't wake up after announcing our arrival.

Kallie, Oiza, Oremeyi, we are home. Wake up guys.

"Oh man, I fell asleep. So happy to be home finally," said Kallie. When he finally woke up. The kids on the other hand were exhausted. My voice fell on deaf ears with them. Right when I was about to raise my voice, Kallie stopped me and suggested we carry them to their rooms.

"I'll get Oiza while you get Oremeyi okay?"

Okay. I'll show you to their rooms.

The kids rooms are connected by a bathroom jack and jill style. I led Kallie to Oiza's room first and went through the connecting bathroom to Oremeyi's room. The kids do not like to sleep in their individual bedrooms but they have no choice tonight. They always make their way to my bedroom during the night. Hopefully, they sleep through the night because someone is taking their spot tonight.

Hey Kallie, are you done tucking Oiza in his bed?

"Yes, I am. I'm just over here admiring his wall decor. Did you put all this on his wall?"

Yes, I did. I thought it was all inspiring.

"It is very nice. I used to have a wallpaper like that race car on my wall when I was a kid too."

That's great, are you ready to go lay down in my bed now?

"Your bed? As in the master suite?"

Yes, the master suite. You have earned your stay tonight, so we might as well take advantage of it before the kids come in there, in the middle of the night.

"I hope they sleep through the night in their own rooms

tonight, so we can cuddle and have the California King bed to ourselves," he said.

I sure hope so too. I have already placed your toothbrush by your sink in the ensuite. Let's go brush our teeth, so you can get in bed, while I go take a shower.

"I would take a shower with you if I wasn't so tired," he teased.

Ha! Wishful thinking Mr. We ain't taking a shower together until you have placed a ring on this finger. I said, wiggling my ring finger.

"Oh woman, trust me, I intend to place a ring on that finger," he answered.

Oh wow! You are really serious about us aren't you?

"Maybe I have not made my intention clear enough but let me try again.

Onyeche, you have made me feel things I never thought were possible and you have brought so much excitement of what the future could hold for us. I used to imagine what life would be like for me when I have a wife and children in the stands, watching my game but whatever I felt does not compare to how I felt today, knowing that you were there today to support me. I want to make you mine, if you would accept me," he said, getting on one knee.

Woah.. what are you doing? I asked while he had one of his hands in his pocket. I watched him reach for his right pocket and pull out a black ring box. I was speechless when I saw the ring he brought out.

"Will you marry me, Onyeche? Because I would love to be your husband and a father to your kids and our future kids. I have heard it said that love can make you do crazy things but I never believed them, until I stumbled across you and the kids in San Diego a week ago."

I stood there speechless for about 60 seconds and then I said;

Kallie, this is crazy. Are you sure you want to do this? I mean, I haven't even told you everything about me yet and your family hasn't met me and my kids.

There are questions that still need to be answered.

"I know this may seem crazy but you make me feel something I have been wanting to feel for the right girl. You brought a whole family to me at a point when I was ready to settle with anyone. You have been so amazing even when you have had no reason to be. Every time I'm around you, all I want to do is be with you and the kids forever. I want to protect you and the kids. I want to be the one who loves you forever and I want to be the one you love forever. Now, I just hope you like the ring and that it fits."

Can you please do this again after we visit your parent's?

"If that is what you want but it still won't make a difference to me because I would choose you again and again. But you can have the next few days to think about it. Please, while you think about it, can I size your ring finger to see if this fits?"

Sure, you can put it on me to see if it fits.

"Why am I shaking while doing this? It fits perfectly. Here's a ring I picked up that I would like for you to put on my finger too."

I took the ring and looked at it and then asked why I should put it on his finger.

"If you want to wait to be engaged to me, that's fine but I don't want to wait to let the world know that I am taken," he answered.

Haha… Alright, I guess it won't hurt to place it on your finger. Kallie had a big smile on his face while I placed the ring on his finger.

You're so mischievous.

I took mine off and handed it back to Kallie and closed the box but he refused to take his ring off.

"I will leave mine on until you accept my proposal and after that, I still won't take it off. I am proud to be called your man and I look forward to being introduced to your family as your fiance. I am also ready to adopt your kids, if you would let me.

Oh wait, what? You are willing to adopt my children and make them yours?

"Yes, I am. They already look like me anyways, why not make it official," he said, winking.

I cannot believe how fast Kallie is willing to work to make us his. Is Kallie on some type of drugs? I probably should've asked before things got this intense between us. Kallie, are you on drugs? Is something wrong with you? "No, I'm not on drugs and nothing is wrong with me. I have just waited a long time to have a woman like you in my life and now that I do, I don't see the reason for wasting time in doing what has to be done. Even the media knows right now that I have a certain amazing woman with two kids whom I call family, in my life."

I don't care about the media Kallie, I care about my heart and my kids. I don't know if you have noticed but I have two kids who might get hurt if you wake up from whatever dream you are currently having. I understand that you are serious about having your own family but why me? Why are you so desperate with me?

"I am sorry if I come off desperate but I won't apologize for the way I feel about you. In all my life, I have never jumped into a relationship with all seriousness like this. I know it may sound weird to you but I feel strongly about you and this started the first night I set my eyes on you." This is really fast but I see how serious you are about us.

"I remember waking up that day in that hotel and saying to myself that this might be the day I meet the woman for me. Just the thought of the possibility of meeting the one for me got me excited and I swear to you, prior to that day, I had been feeling a little out of my element and lonely. Having a family of my own is something I am really serious about. Before I met you, I had been on a few dates but nothing was serious.

I'd be lying if I told you that there aren't a lot of girls waiting to literally throw themselves at me but I have never felt this way towards anyone but you," he explained.

Why me of all people? Couldn't you have fallen for one of

the gorgeous women waiting to capture your heart? I saw that one lady with really large boobs shaking them in your face at the stadium today. Why not her?

"Oh God, hell no. She was being rude first of all and secondly I already have the woman for me," he said

And who might the woman for you be?

"You, of course. I love you and I love your kids. I don't mind stepping into a father role with them and being the type of father and husband you deserve.

I don't know if you have noticed but women like you are rare to find and I am not going to give up the chance to have you. You know, I hate the jerk that treated you badly but he was a fool to have never seen what a rare gem you are. I am a man who sees things clearly, especially when it comes to a rare gem like you, Onyeche. You are amazing and I would be crazy to mess things up with you."

Thank you for your vote of confidence Kallie but I don't know if I want to allow myself to be messed with again. Things would have been different if I didn't have kids whom I adore, but I have kids and they are the center of my universe. I feel it as my life's calling to give them the best of me. In order for anyone to have a shot at a relationship with me, I think it is fair that they know that my children will always come first and I will never neglect them for anyone.

"This is exactly how I knew that I struck a rare gem with you. You speak your mind and lay it out there like it is. I love that about you and God knows I would never want you to put me ahead of the kids. Matter of fact, I am willing to put the kids first also. I am ready to rise to the occasion in whatever way I have to, in order to make things work for us all," said Kallie.

I must be crazy to say what I am about to say but I think it is only fair to let you know that I am falling for you too. If I was the old naive girl I used to be, I would say nothing could ever make me walk away from you but I am not naive and neither am I controlled by my emotions like I used to be. Having kids has helped me learn to build boundaries around my life in order to keep myself and my kids safe from trashy situations. Can you please take off that ring for now? I asked, changing the topic.

"Why should I? You don't want to accept my proposal but I accepted yours," he said with a mischievous smile and began to run around the bedroom anticipating me to chase him. I chased him around for a bit and then gave up. You make me happy Kallie and you are a big kid too. I can't believe I have another kid to chase around also. I shook my head and said dear Lord help me.

Kallie walked toward me and held both my hands in each of his, looked me in my eyes and said I was the answer to his prayer and that he would do everything he could to convince me that all he wants is to make me and the kids happy.

"You may have just come into my life, but you have changed it forever. When I am with you, the world and all the distractions cease to exist. There is a peace and quiet that surrounds you that I love.You are my dream come true, girl."

Wow! Kallie, you really do have a way with words, don't you? I enjoy your company too and it is fun cooking for more than just me and the kids. I do enjoy the excitement that you bring to our lives.

Tuesday morning before you left for Denver. It was crazy how someone said they had just sighted you at a bar with a big breasted brunette and I said I must be that brunette then. The time they claimed they saw you, you were here playing with the kids.

"See, most of the articles written about celebrities are lies to help the papers and sites sell their story. I am also very happy that you have not turned out to be a phony either. It is crazy how hard it is these days to find sincere people. The more I talk to you and spend time with you, the more convinced I am that I want to marry you. By the way, which country is your accent from?"

See, this is one of many serious questions I was hoping you would ask me since the day we met. I was born and raised in Nigeria, in a little city called Kontagora. Let's just say I'm a Northern girl from Nigeria. What else do you want to know about me?

"Wow! Interesting that the Queen of my heart is from the motherland. How did you come to America? What made you come to America?"

Growing up in the North, my parents only supported my education until high school. After that, I was on my own. I knew I wanted to get more education than just high school and I was interested in travelling overseas to get a degree. Knowing the kind of family that I came from, there was no way studying abroad was possible. My parents didn't know anyone abroad nor would they make such a huge financial sacrifice for me.

I went to my dad one day and told him I wanted to pursue my studies abroad and make large sums of money so I could help take care of him and my mom. While he loved the idea of me taking care of them, he said I was crazy for dreaming that big.

KALLIE

What happened after that and how did you make it to the states?

"It was easy for me to give up on that dream but I don't give up easily on something I care about. I remember visualizing myself overseas studying amongst people who spoke American slang all day long. It makes me smile now, just thinking about my dreams.

One day on my way from a friend's house, I spotted an American Oyibo (white person) like you, trying so hard to speak Hausa to a grocer at a kiosk near where my friends lived. I stopped and asked him what he wanted. He told me he wanted some sugar, so I became his interpreter. After helping him with his grocery, he asked if I was interested in travelling to America on an exchange study program and I said yes. It turned out he was a recruiter from a reputable college in the US. He helped me get everything I needed and that was how my life changed," she concluded.

Wow, what a story! I still want to hear some more but you need to get in the shower babe. Sorry for keeping you hostage for this long.

I looked at the gigantic wall clock in the bedroom and it was already 1:00 am in the morning. Time sure flies when you are having a great time.

"I can't believe it is already 1:00 AM in the morning. I have to get a quick shower so we can go to sleep. Sorry for keeping you up past your bedtime Kallie. I'm sure if you weren't here, you'd already be in bed snoring loudly," she teased.

Well, thanks for the thought but being with you makes life fun and energizing. Alright get your fine self into the shower before you make me get in there with you. She ran off into the bathroom and turned the shower on. I heard it run for 15 minutes and then heard her turn it off.

She came into the bedroom smelling fresh and looking like a goddess in her silk metallic grey nightgown.

You look nice and beautiful in your nightgown, my Queen. I'll try not to grope you when you are laying in my arms.

"Are you going to bed with your pants and t-shirt on?"

I was going to but now that you mentioned it, I'll lose everything except for my boxers if that is okay with you. Normally, I sleep in my boxers but I was trying to be a gentleman.

"Sleep in whatever feels comfortable to you Kallie. You are already in my bed, you might as well be as comfortable as you can but please don't sleep bare ass," she advised.

Bare ass? Have you been thinking about my ass woman? I asked because I wanted to see her reaction. She just giggled and said

"your boxers stay on."

I woke up to the delicious smell of bacon and it was so inviting. Once again, I looked to the left at the bedside table and as I had expected, a note was waiting for me.

"Waking up to you this morning was amazing. If you are reading this, bring your sexy self to the kitchen and eat some breakfast."

What is there not to love about this amazing woman? She is the real deal and I am so ready to make her mine. I just need to let her move at her own pace and I hope her pace catches up to mine soon.

I feel so good after a long night's rest and I don't remember what happened the rest of the night. As soon as I closed my eyes, I was gone. Her bed is so comfortable and I didn't want to get up from it but eating with the family is more important to me than being a lazy Ass this morning.

I got up and headed to the bathroom to pee and then brush my teeth. She had my brush and toothpaste placed on a clean plush golden towel. It felt like I was at a luxury hotel.

Goodmorning family, sorry I overslept.

"Good morning Kallie, you took our spot last night," said Oiza.

Oh buddy I'm sorry but I really enjoyed your spot. I said with a smile. Oiza made it clear he didn't like that I took their spot.

Hey princess, how are you today?

"I'm fine, how about you?" She asked me.

I'm great and I smell bacon. Princess was already eating two pieces of crispy bacon on her plate.

"Hey boy, did you have a goodnight?" Asked the Queen of the castle.

I sure did. When I rolled over to your side and didn't find you, I was about to wonder where you were and then I smelled bacon. I got up and traced the smell of bacon to find you here.

"Yes, I sent the smell of bacon your way on purpose. Did you read my note?" She asked. Yes, my lady and I loved it. Did you sleep through the night with me or did the kids come into the bedroom late at night?

"I slept till 4:00 am and yes the kids came in and I walked them back to their rooms but we all ended up sleeping in Oiza's room for the rest of the night," she explained.

Wow, the kids didn't let you spend the whole time with me huh? Oh boy! I got a real competition and I can't complain because it's pretty clear the kids have me beat on this one.

"Yeah, they do. They complained about not sleeping in their spots. They almost kicked you off the bed but I pleaded with them and also reminded them of the toys you got them," she explained.

Did any of that work?

"Well, it did for a bit. You are still here aren't you?" She asked, smiling.

I guess so and I am freaking happy to still be here. Wow! Woman, you have made a whole lot like last time. Do you always cook this much or is it because of me?

"Only when I have someone else to feed also. I hope you enjoy breakfast."

Oh you bet I will. You are amazing and I am so glad I get to spend this time with the most amazing woman and mom I have ever known.

"Aww, please don't make me cry. Being a mom is the best thing that ever happened to me and each passing day I remind myself of how grateful I am to have my little ones," she added.

I know how you feel to an extent because I feel the love you have for them and me. I would be honored and be the luckiest man in the world when you finally accept my marriage proposal.

"Haha… I am glad you know that I am a loving person. Can we eat now?" She asked, terminating the conversation.

Absolutely, I don't want the food to get cold before we enjoy it.

ONYECHE

Today, we fly out to Michigan to meet Kallie's family and I am a little nervous. I have never travelled on a whim like this to meet anyone's parents before. I wonder what his parents and siblings would think about me and the kids. Perhaps it is a bad idea for me to focus on what they might think or say but I cannot help it.

Knowing Kallie, these past few days have been amazing and I have sort of grown accustomed to having a strong, caring, loving and sexy man around me.

He has such a manly presence that I love and I don't know what I would do if things don't work out between us. "Girl, you are way stronger than you are giving yourself credit for. If anything happens, you will be fine and still thrive," said my inner voice. I know I'll be fine but it's been a while since someone has shown this much commitment to me and expressed such intense interest in being a part of my life. Kallie is such a great catch and is way more accomplished than all the men I have ever dated or married. While the other guys I had dated and married made me feel like they were the better ones in the relationship after all my sacrifice, yet here's a man who has way more than I imagined for my dream man, begging for my yes.

In life, in order to enjoy something better, we have to be open to it. Risk-taking is important in order to get what you have never gotten before, though there's this looming fear that it might not work out. Why am I suddenly philosophizing?

As I make this journey with Kallie today, I choose to keep my heart open and enjoy the journey and experience. I make myself a promise to not judge or have any expectations but deal with every situation that arises as it arises.

"Are you excited to meet my folks?" He asked.

Yes I am and am also nervous as hell at the same time. How long are we going to be there for?

"I was thinking 3-4 days. That way they really get to know you and the kids better and see what I see in you. My parents are crazy about grandkids and I have no doubt Oiza and Princess will be spoiled this week," he said with excitement.

Like they aren't already spoiled enough. Did you book us a hotel near your parent's place?

"Nope, we are staying at their home," he announced.

What?! Isn't that too much?

"No it's not. They insisted. Moreover, they have a 10 bedroom home and prefer that we stay with them. I didn't tell you this but I told them to prepare rooms that are close together because you wouldn't want the kids to be away from you and they said they would do just that," he explained.

Thank you babe, you are amazing.

"My pleasure and anything for you."

Our flight to Michigan took two hours and 35 minutes. Kallie and I spent it talking about what to expect and how excited his parents were to host us for the next three to four days. He flew us first class on Delta Airlines. I don't know how Kallie does it but for a superstar of his caliber, his fans don't jump all over him, they kind of keep a little bit of distance, like they are aware he values his privacy. The ones who recognized him on the flight, let him know how proud they were of his last performance at the Mountain Lions stadium.

Kallie expressed his gratitude while making sure Oiza and Princess were secured and protected as much as possible. When we stepped out of the airport, there was a black Escalade waiting to pick us up.

A white haired man and his wife stepped out almost at the same time. The man came out of the drivers' seat, while the wife from the front passenger seat with open arms to meet Kallie. Kallie's dad reached for him with open arms while the mom reached for me and gave me a big hug. She said she was happy to finally meet me and then almost simultaneously, they ignored me and Kallie and reached for Oiza and Oremeyi.

"Awww look at these adorable two. We are happy to meet you two," they said while embracing each child.

"I hope you are hungry because we have plenty to eat at home," said Heidi; Kallie's mom.
Nice to meet you Mr and Mrs Goodall.

"It is finally great to meet the woman who has captured our son's heart," replied Mr John Goodall.

"Thank you for agreeing to meet us this soon, we truly are grateful for that," said Mrs Heidi Goodall.

I am glad you invited us over because I couldn't wait to meet the ones who raised this amazing man right here.

"We are very proud of our son, he makes us so happy," answered Mrs Goodall. After settling in for about a couple of hours, Kallie came to let me know that his parents wanted to talk to me.

"Babe, my parents would like to talk to you for a bit. Hope you don't mind?" He asked. I'm happy to talk to them. How about the kids? Where would they be while I'm talking to your parents?

"Oh babe, don't worry about the kids. I will keep them entertained and also make sure that they have a lot to eat and drink while you chat with my parents," he answered.

Okay, why do they want to chat this early? We just got here.

Am I supposed to be scared? Oh Kallie, what if it gets awkward?

"Knowing you, it will go great. Just be yourself and be honest with your answers and all should go well," he encouraged me.

I will try to be myself and thanks for the vote of confidence in me. Where are they right now?

"They are in their office, right over there," he said, pointing at a study next to the foyer. Wish me luck. I said as I made my way to the study.

"Hello Onyeche, we are very happy that you could join us today. Please take a seat," offered Mr Goodall.

Thank you sir, it's an honor to finally meet you and thank you for inviting me and my kids into your beautiful home.

"Oh no worries. You are always welcome here," said Mrs Goodall.

"So, my son expressed his interest in you to us and we are very excited to learn more about you for ourselves. We see that you obviously have kids and there must have been someone else in your life prior to meeting our son," Mr Goodall said, going straight to the point.

Yes, I was married before but it ended and I have my kids to raise and I am happy.

"Our son expressed to us that you are being hesitant in accepting his proposal. Is that true?" Mrs Goodall asked.

Yes I am and the reason is because we just met a few weeks ago and your son thinks I'm his soulmate and wants me to be his wife. I have never experienced anyone as forthcoming as your son and I have some concerns.

"Our son has never been this serious about a woman before until now. We don't mean to say that he has never had serious relationships but he has never connected with another's spirit as much as he connects with yours," explained Mrs Goodall.

Your son is a superstar athlete and thousands of women would gladly jump at the opportunity to be with him. Yet he chooses me? Please don't get me wrong, I know I am amazing but I have never seen or heard of a celebrity who wants to be with a woman who already has kids and is willing to adopt her kids and give them his name. I guess all I am trying to say is that I have my kids to think about. If I get hurt and I'm not saying that Kallie would hurt me, but if I did, it won't be just me but my kids also who will be hurt and I don't know how I would deal with that.

"Oh dear, you have nothing to be afraid of with Kallie. Moreover, I believe this has Divine timing to it. I don't mean to weird you out, but I was visiting with one of my SEER friends a few weeks back and she mentioned something about my son meeting a woman out of the ordinary who would turn out to be an extraordinary part of his life. She went on to say that she comes with two amazing gifts Divinely sent to fill the void my son has. Of course, I didn't understand all that she was saying until Kallie called us to let us know he would be bringing someone to see us and two little ones also," explained Mrs Goodall.

About the SEER, Mrs Goodall I am not weirded out because I pray and meditate and I believe God reveals things to us directly and sometimes to others for our benefit. However, I also know that God has given me a brain to be able to think and reason things through as well.

"What are you afraid of? Why do I feel like you are trying to convince yourself not to open up to Kallie for the fear that you might get hurt again?"

Mr Goodall asked and that was when I thought it hit me hard.

I think I'm afraid of letting my heart open again and be hurt.

"Our son would never hurt you. Besides, in life you have to take risks because without them, you never truly live like you were meant to. I don't know if Kallie already told you this but when I first came across that social media post about you two being seen at the San Diego Zoo, I thought to myself 'wow she is beautiful and her kids look like my son.' Of course I called him to find out if he had been seeing you secretly and had kids that we didn't know about. He said he didn't want to talk about it until we saw each other in person," said Mr Goodall.

I thought that when you saw that post, you would be judging the gold digger that was pictured with your son.

"Oh no dear, we like to give people the benefit of the doubt. We did wonder for a second what was going on but we trust our son," replied Mrs Goodall.

How do you guys feel about me being African and a single mom?

"Oh honey, we don't care about where you are from and how many kids you have. None of these count but that you are a decent, caring and loving person. From what we have heard about you from our son, we are happy he found a rare gem like you," she added.

"To add to that honey, we read some disturbing articles about you recently but we didn't take it to heart because we know these people would write anything to get attention. We just hope that you and Kallie focus on each other and the kids and ignore all else because what matters is family," said Mr Goodall.

You guys are like the best parents ever. Here I was thinking that you guys were going to give me a reason to walk away but here you are encouraging me to stay instead.

"We know he can make you and the kids happy. Honey, I understand that this may sound contrary to what most parents would do but we are not most people and we trust our son," added Mrs Goodall.

"Honey, we will treat your kids as part of the family and never give you a reason to doubt our love for them as one of our grandkids. They will never feel left out and we promise this to you with God as our witness," swore Mr Goodall.

Sir, you didn't have to swear to me. I believe you and I would be crazy not to want to be a part of your family. Has Kallie told you anything about my parents?

"No, honey, we really don't want to interfere in your personal business. Well, since you asked. Are your parents okay with you and Kallie?"

I have not told them anything about Kallie yet and honestly, they don't care who I marry because they are not going to live with me. They expect me to make decisions that are right for me.

"That's great advice and they sound like they are good people," added Mrs Goodall.

They are when they want to be.

"We will be very happy to meet your parents whenever you and Kallie think it is right," added Mr Goodall.

I am still amazed at my conversation with Kallie's parents. They practically proposed on behalf of their son. They wanted me to know that they trust their son and believe he would be a great partner and father and they also promised to treat my kids as one of their grandkids. I find myself asking what just happened? I went into that conversation hoping for things to go out of control and be uncomfortable but instead, I found myself being encouraged to take a leap of faith and give Kallie a chance. I still find it crazy that the most amazing people I have ever met are the ones trying to give me a reason to take a chance at again.

KALLIE

Hey babe, how did it go with my parents?

"It went better than I had expected," she replied.

See, I told you there was nothing for you to worry about.

"I know but it's crazy how happy they are for us and gave me reasons to give myself a chance at love again," she answered.

My parents are very understanding and they have experience with love. I trust them and knew that they would be there for me when I finally introduced the woman I love to them.

"So, who is this woman that you love?"

You are the woman that I love. I love you so much and would be blessed to have you in my life. I hope that if you had any doubts, you were able to put them to rest after speaking with my parents.

"Your mom mentioned something to me about visiting with her SEER friend and was told you would meet a woman who would come with two wonderful gifts that would win your heart over?" She asked, squinting.

Oh dear God, I told my mom not to mention that at all. Talk about trying to spoil my chances.

"She is not trying to spoil your chances Kallie. I actually thought that it was sweet that she mentioned it. Although I made it clear to her that while I believe God reveals things to us through others, He also gave us a brain to choose what is right for us," she explained.

You are absolutely right. I believe that God brings situations into our lives to help us see how he has been working something out in the background, even when we may not really see it. If our union is Divinely ordained, I am completely open to seeing how it all unfolds but first, I need to know how you are feeling.

"Well since you asked, I am feeling really good about everything. Your parents seem genuinely nice and open to seeing us together. They seem more supportive than I thought they would be and they didn't even ask if I was after your money or security for me and my kids. They definitely surprised me.

"I am glad that you now see the fallacy of expecting the worst. So, would you please marry me now? I asked, getting on one knee. I didn't pay attention to the surroundings because all I wanted was to hear her say yes.

"Kallie, please get up. Can we do this later? Your parents are watching us and I'm nervous," she responded.

I won't get up until you say yes. While I was waiting for her to say yes, the kids came out of the play area and knelt down with me, asking their mama to marry me because they would love to have me as their daddy.

"Kallie, before I say yes to you, I must first warn you. My 'yes' carries a lot of promise and weight and that I don't take lightly. Saying yes to you means opening up my heart again, knowing that I might get hurt again. Are you really sure you want to do this? Marriage is a big deal.'

I already know that and I am willing to take that leap.

You are walking into this knowing that you become an instant dad and have fatherly duties and responsibilities that you will have to step into immediately. Is this really what you want?" She asked.

Yes, I understand the responsibility of being a parent and a husband and there's no one else I would rather share that with than you. Marrying you is something I would do a thousand times if it means waking up to you and these babies every morning. So please say yes before I hurt my knee from kneeling for so long.

"Yes!" She answered.

She said yes and I couldn't believe it. I jumped up and lifted her up in the air.

I am going to make you the happiest woman alive everyday from today babe. You deserve a man who would worship the very ground you walk on and I promise I'm that man. I turned and pulled the kids into the hug with us because they definitely surprised me. I had no idea they were going to assist me in convincing their mama to give me a chance.

My parents joined in to congratulate us on our engagement and my mom was able to sneak a picture in too. She captured the moment the kids knelt down with me asking their mama to give me a chance.

"Thank you so much Mr and Mrs Goodall for welcoming us into your home and family," said Onyeche.

"Oh we are very happy to have you be a part of the family. Congrats son, you couldn't have chosen a better woman to be a part of the family," said Mrs Goodall.

Thank you mom for the support. Dad, thank you for showing me how to go for what I want in spite of the obstacles in my way. I owe this moment to the two of you and my son and daughter.

"Mama is Kallie going to be our new daddy?" Asked Oiza.

"I guess so baby. Are you happy with that?" She asked him.

"Yes, mama. He is amazing and I can't wait to call him dad," he added.

Today has been a really good day for me and I can't wait for what the rest of our lives hold together.

The next day, my mom asked if I wouldn't mind an engagement party.

"Son, do you want us to organize an engagement party before you leave for Colorado springs?"

No mum, you don't need to but I'll ask Onyeche if she wouldn't mind. I'll leave it up to her to make the decision.

"I totally understand son," said mom.

Whatever she decides, we will be fine with it."

Aww mom, thank you so much for being so kind and sweet.

"You're welcome son. We can tell that you both adore each other and we believe you will make an amazing couple."

I can only say that having you and dad as examples make it easy for me to want the same for myself and my girl.I wanted a family and a woman who would be there for me and really see me like you see dad and I believe that I have found her. She is different from all the others I have dated and since the first day we met her, after spending a few hours with her, all I wanted to do was marry her. I never thought that I would be the kind of person who would ask a woman to marry him after only a few days together but here we are and I would break my rule again and again just for her.

"Aww son, that right there is how you know you've found your person."

ONYECHE

We have been at Kallie's parents for a couple of days now and everyday has been a party. Kallie had asked me if it was okay if his parents organized an engagement party for us and I told him they didn't have to. He said he already knew that I would say that, so he'd warned his parents before asking me.

"My parents are okay either way. They wanted me to tell you that they would be fine either way. They are just so happy that we found each other and are now engaged," he explained.

After lunch with Kallie and his parents that afternoon, he left to go pick up his sister and her family from the airport. Kallie's brother Ian came by that morning to have breakfast with us. He seemed really nice.

I am engaged! It is wild and crazy that I would be in this position with the best man I could ever ask for. I don't think Kallie understands the magnitude of what marrying an African entails especially when the parents of the bride find out he is a wealthy man. My parents were particularly not happy with my first marriage because my ex was not super rich and wouldn't send them money when they requested it. I had tried to send them money as much as I could but it was enough. They always wanted more.

It broke my heart each time I tried to check on them but never really felt like they cared for me. They don't even call me to ask about the kids genuinely without asking for money in the same sentence. So when my marriage ended, they could care less. They haven't even called to check on how me and the kids are doing in a while. I remember reaching out to them for assistance once but they turned me down. They said I was the one who was supposed to send them money since I live in the land of money, not the other way around.

My siblings have not been completely helpful either. Last time I heard, they were all laughing at me for what happened to me and even wished that I hadn't survived the heartbreak. I know it sounds heartless what they did and still do but I have been kind to them.

The worst didn't happen after my divorce instead better things started coming to me.

I should warn Kallie before I introduce him to them. I will have to set some boundaries because I am wiser and I know better now.

Forty five minutes later Kallie returned from the airport.

"Hey babe, I would love for you to meet my sister Evelyn and her husband Jay and their two little ones Eve and Jaylen," he said.

Hi, nice to meet you. I have heard so many amazing things about you all.

"You are so pretty. We are happy to meet the woman who is finally going to tame the Beast," said Evelyn.

Haha thank you. You have such adorable kids.

"Thank you, we love them very much," answered Jay.

"Hey mama, we are hungry," said Oiza.

"Hey little man, how are you?" Asked Jay.

"I'm fine. How are you?" Asked Oiza.

"We are fine. We are happy to meet you and also brought you some friends. Meet Eve and Jaylen," said Evelyn.

The kids looked at one another, smiled and ran off together, towards the play area. They warmed up to one another faster than I had expected.

"Well I guess the kids are now best friends," said Jay, running off to supervise them.

"I want you to know that you are welcome to our home anytime. You and the kids can come by and spend holidays and weekends with us," invited Evelyn.

"Hey, how about me?" Asked Kallie.

"You are welcome to join too. Onyeche, has he told you how obsessed he is with his niece and nephew?"

Yes, he has told me how much he loves spending time with them.

"I must tell you, you got a great man in my brother, please treat him right," she said, walking off.

I promise I will. It was nice meeting you again Mrs. Evelyn. I said, as she walked to the kids. Kallie had walked away earlier to talk to Mr. Jay, while I was speaking with his sister.

I have to talk to Kallie about my family and what I really want for my next wedding. The great thing about us is that we have been very honest with each other since we started our relationship. No matter how many people we have around us, life is always going to be about the two of us and how we treat each other. We are not going to live with family members or dictate our lives based on their preference or expectations but ours. I have made it clear to Kallie that I don't live my life anymore trying to meet other people's expectations because that never ends well. I remember how disappointed my parents were in me whenever I didn't send them as much money as they'd expected from me. They complained and said I should have at least married someone richer so I could send them more money. I remember very well how they made it seem like I was an investment or insurance ticket for their future. I hope to explain some of these to Kallie soon because he is obviously the dream of every selfish African parent whose intention it is to benefit from their daughter's marriage. This is my chance to set some boundaries.

Hey Kallie, can we talk?

"Is everything okay babe?"

Yes, everything is fine but there is something important I

have to share with you about my parents.

"Okay, babe, I'm listening."

Well, I grew up thinking that I was my parents' investment.

"I don't understand all of this babe."

Growing up, they reminded me that I was an investment they intended to cash in when the time was right. They always laid emphasis on my attitude. Whenever I'd act silly, they often reminded me that no rich man would want to marry me.

" Is there anything specific you are trying to tell me?"

Yes, my parents reminded me more than one billion times when I was growing up that I was an investment and they must reap from their labor. What that means is I am expected to give them everything they ask for and I don't like that at all. It doesn't matter if meeting their needs means that I won't have enough for my own needs.Though I have been very generous with them in the past, even when I didn't have to be. Yet they never call to check on me or the kids, unless they need money. I used to wish that they would call me to check on how I was doing without asking for something in the same phone call. I tried the best I could in the past to meet their demands but it was never enough. Hence, I made up my mind to not fall for their tricks anymore and now I say no, whenever they ask me for money. I have learned to intentionally cut our conversations short whenever they call because I know their intention is to take from me.

"What do you want me to do with this information?"

Babe, here's where this applies to you, you are rich and when they find out, they would want you to give them the world.

"Why would I give them the world?"

In the African culture I grew up in, the man pays a bride price and the amount of money you pay is dependent on how rich you are. Knowing how they are, I'd expect them to start calling me more often when they hear about my engagement to you and I also expect to start hearing about relatives I never knew about until now because of your financial status.

"I still don't get what you are trying to tell me babe," he

said.

Here's what I am trying to say; you are not going to spend any money on them unless you want to and I promise to never ask you to give them money. I want boundaries between you and them and please promise me that you will always be open with me, if they somehow try to sneak their way to you.

"I promise babe and thank you for opening up to me. I know it must be hard being vulnerable for a strong woman like you and I appreciate your honesty very much. However, I don't want you to worry about them or anyone else sneaking their way to me. I will always go through you before I make any decisions or do anything for them. I look forward to meeting them soon because I don't want to be engaged forever. I want to marry you as soon as possible," he said.

He took it better than I thought and I was thankful for his response.

Thank you for your understanding babe. I don't want a long engagement either. I even thought of asking you to elope with me and do a court wedding, so we can have sex afterward and plan a big reception for the family later. What do you think about that?

"I think we should have sex right now, if you feel like it. We don't have to elope to make love. But I respect your decision to wait until we are married. I only hope that I don't get blue balls when that time comes and you leave me because I can't satisfy you in bed," he joked.

Haha funny. You won't develop blue balls and I'm not going anywhere babe. I'm pretty sure you can satisfy an African woman in bed.

"I hope so babe, because it would hurt my feelings if I'm not able to keep up with you in bed. I'm pretty sure that I will make you fall deeper in love after making love to you," he teased.

Alright tiger, I hear you. I'm looking forward to officially calling you my husband though. "Me too because then you can completely open up and let me guard your heart with the very air I breathe babe," he promised.

I didn't know you were a poet too, babe. By the way, one more thing you need to know; my parents still live in Kontagora, Nigeria. What do you think about flying out there to see them as soon as we are able to?

"Sure, would my off season be okay?" He asked.

That's in a couple of months and that would be more than okay.

"Sounds like a plan but I don't want to wait that long before I make love to you though," he added.

What should we do, babe?

"Well, I don't want you to do it because you feel forced or guilty. I understand that you want to wait and I truly respect that and I would be lying if I said I haven't wanted to have sex since the first day we met. Not to say if you had slept with me earlier it would have changed anything or made me love you any less," he explained.

Thank you for that honest disclosure Mr. Kallie. Now, can I get a sensual kiss that will make my vagina sing?

"Haha…What a tease! Yes you can, my lady." As soon as our lips touched, my whole body collapsed into his embrace.

It was like finally coming home to the one you love. The kiss was intimate and sensual. It was deeper than any other kiss we had shared up to that moment. I felt my vagina contract and my nipples harden against his chest and I could feel Kallie's hardness crushing against my belly. It took every ounce of control in me not to drag him to the bedroom and make love to him. When we separated our lips, Kallie's grey eyes seemed like a storm of dark grey clouds mixed with blue. This man is sexy as hell and he makes my body quake whenever we kiss and I love revelling in his male beauty with my eyes. I love running my hands down his hard muscular body too.

"You are such a beautiful woman and you make me want to explode in you. I have never met a woman who made me wait until you. I don't remember meeting anyone who could set me on fire by just looking at me until you. You're one of a kind and I promise to be devoted to you for as long as I live," he promised.

Babe, that would make an amazing wedding vow. You set my whole body and soul on fire too babe. I am still trying to rationalize how it is that I got you. For I have never met a man who opened up to me like you did and who jumped all in at once without holding back. I used to think that men like you didn't exist. Never thought in a thousand years that I would be blessed to meet one or even have one until you. It still feels like a dream to me. Ouch, Kallie. I didn't mean you should pinch me. "Now you know that I am real," he said, laughing.

KALLIE

The time we spent with my parents in Minnesota was great. They obviously loved meeting my lady and the kids. The kids didn't want to leave when it was time to go. They enjoyed playing with Eve and Jaylen a lot. I must be one of the luckiest men alive to be engaged to an amazing woman like Onyeche. I couldn't believe how supportive the kids were in my proposal. I am so grateful to my parents for their support and love also.

Now I look forward to going to Nigeria and meeting my wife's family. This upcoming off season will be really exciting and I am ready for it.

We have been in Colorado Springs for about three hours and I feel like going out to dinner with the family.

Hey babe, would you mind going out to a steakhouse to eat dinner tonight?

"Babe, I don't mind but I think I'll cook us dinner tonight," she offered.

Babe, you really don't have to and I don't want you to think that I expect you to always cook and clean or do my laundry. We can hire someone to handle all that for us. I am happy to be with you babe and will not mind if you don't cook ever.

"I am happy to make dinner for us babe. We can hire someone to help sometimes but not all the time. I have become so used to taking care of the kids and doing everything by myself that it will take me a second to adjust to having someone help me. However, I am willing to give it a try," she answered.

Good, I'm glad you are willing to give it a try. So are we going out to dinner tonight? "Nope. We are eating at home. Are you not about to review your game tape that the coach sent you?"

Yes babe but I was planning to do that later in the basement tonight, while the kids are asleep. I want to make sure I don't get distracted because it is important I take notes while watching it.

"That's great babe. I'll make sure the basement is ready for you and you have all the space you need to review your game tape okay?"

You're the best!

"Aww you're welcome, sexy. Can you chop vegetables?"

Yes, I can. Do you need some help?

"Yes, I need these lettuce and carrots chopped for me. The knife is sharp, please be careful."

I will babe. I love spending time with you. This is better than I ever dreamed it would be. Me and my wife, cooking dinner together and having a conversation in the kitchen. I didn't even think that I would marry a woman who could cook. You make me feel so lucky.

"You make me feel lucky and I was not even looking to be lucky or meeting anyone but here we are."

I am glad that I showed up even though you were not looking.

About an hour and thirty minutes later dinner was ready and we had another amazing home cooked meal.

You always amaze me with how delicious your food tastes. I can't wait to taste the other food.

"Really Kallie, you had to say that with the kids right here."

I'm sorry but I really like your food. I responded with a smile. I honestly didn't mean to be rude around the kids and thankfully, they don't know what we are talking about.

"Yes, thank God. I want my kids to be kids as long as they

can," she added.

By the way, I got you an NFL League Pass, so you can watch the games you and the kids won't be able to make in person.

"Awww that is so nice of you, babe.

Is this how my life is going to be now? Full of surprises and gifts?"

Yes and you should start getting used to it. I understand that the kids are young and you can't always be present at all the games but you can cheer me on from home.

"I'd like to go to all the games," announced Oiza.

"Me too," added Oremeyi.

I wish you could come to all the games too kiddos but I'll be happy if you stayed home sometimes and watch me play from home.

"Thanks for being so understanding," said Onyeche.

You're welcome my love.

After dinner, the kids went off to play and I stayed to help Onyeche clean up the kitchen. I have never had a problem helping out in the kitchen. Even as a child, my mom said I was always happy to assist her in the kitchen. "You are amazing and I'm so happy our kids have a great role model in you, babe."

You're welcome.

The kids are now in bed and I am ready to go and review my game tape in the basement. I had no idea this house could be any bigger. The basement is like a big game room with a 75 inch screen planted on the wall. My lady made sure I had everything I needed and more. The room was quiet and I had some popcorn, two bottled water and a few pens kept on the coffee table for me with a notepad for note taking. I was in such a hurry to review the tape that I forgot my notepad upstairs. I swear, this woman already knows me inside out and it only seems to get better. I don't think I have ever been with a woman who plans ahead like Onyeche does.

ONYECHE

Hello mama and papa. How are you guys doing today?
"We are doing well now that you remembered to call us," answered mama.

I am fine and the kids are doing well too. I added that part knowing they wouldn't ask.

"Oh my grandchildren, how are they doing?" Asked mama.

They are doing well, thank you for asking.

"How is your husband and have you guys settled yet?" Asked papa.

No, we have not settled and we are divorced. I already told you guys about the whole situation but you somehow still think I need to go back to him?

"We know better than you know about life. If we ask you to go back it is because we see life more clearly than you.

We spoke with a mallam who told us God told him to ask you to go back and beg your husband to take you back," said mama.

Over my dead body mama. We are already divorced and nothing will ever make me go back. Anyways, the reason I called is to let you know that I am getting married soon and I will be bringing my future husband for my introduction soon.

"Which husband? What is going on here?" Asked papa.

I am getting married again and he wants to come by and do the introduction and traditional wedding.

"Okay. Who is he, what does he do for a living and where is he from?" Asked mama.

He is from Minnesota, USA and he plays football for a living.

"Is he rich and can he take care of you and the children?" Asked papa.

It doesn't matter if he is rich and I can take care of myself and my children without any man's help. I love him and he is a good man and he loves my kids as his own. We are thinking about coming by next month to see you all.

"You did not answer our question about your new husband. Is he rich and capable?" Insisted mama.

He is not poor and how much money he has shouldn't concern you because you are not the one marrying him.

I didn't mean to be rude but my parents are very aggravating. This is why I rarely call them and only speak briefly with them when I do. They really don't care for anything else but money and it sucks.

"Have you told your sisters that you are getting married again?" Asked mama.

No, I have not. I wanted to let you know first and then we can start planning.

"Okay. Make sure you let your husband know that we expect dowry and other things from him," added papa.

I already told him that.

"We are excited to meet him but you know you need to send some money to prepare before you get here right?" Said papa.

I know and that is why I already sent you $5,000 to get what you need before we visit.

"Oh thank you so much our daughter. You are the best daughter in the world," said papa. You are welcome papa and I will see you all in four weeks.

I ended the call feeling a little down but hopeful. I was a little disappointed but didn't let it get to me. I've often wondered if other people's parents are like mine but I will not let myself worry too much about that. After all, I have an amazing man who cares for me and my kids and that is all that counts. I am also grateful that I am no longer the naive and gullible woman I used to be. One that my parents and others could manipulate easily.

Are you ready to meet my family babe?

"Yes, I am. I can't wait to get the ball rolling with us," said Kallie with excitement.

Once again congrats on winning the Superbowl babe.

"Thank you, my love. It was your presence in my life that brought me good luck," he added.

I am so proud of you and all that you have achieved within such a short time babe.

You were also named MVP of the Super Bowl and the NFL regular season in addition to breaking multiple passing yard records and touchdowns. The kids and I are so happy we have you.

"I am very happy to have you and the kids too and now that we are going to meet your parents and have our traditional wedding in Nigeria, life couldn't be any better," he added.

I hope you are ready for the craziness babe. It's about to be wild and loud. I'm happy that your family and friends are coming too. It should be great.

"One of my friends is already asking if there might be a woman waiting for him in your hometown babe," he added.

There will most definitely be a lot of women wanting to be connected to your friends. I hope they get lucky but I don't want to get in the middle of anything because this is my time and I intend to enjoy it without worrying about setting up your friends.

"I'm sorry babe, I didn't mean to sound like I wanted you to play matchmaker. This is your moment and I will make sure everyone respects your wishes," he said, thoughtfully.

Good, you are always so thoughtful, babe. I have spoken with the tailor working on our African traditional clothes and he said everything is ready and they even made extra clothes as directed, for your friends.

"That sounds amazing. I can't wait to dress like an African chief at our traditional wedding."

Haha… you are so funny and yes, you will make a very sexy African chief. I can't believe that all of the magazines I grew up reading such as The Ovation, This Day Style and another one I can't remember right now will be there. It is so crazy that I didn't even have to invite them myself. Thanks to one of my sisters, they offered to come by with their amazing photographers.

"That's wonderful, babe. I can't believe we will be there in a couple of days,"

Yes we will and I am excited for it.

Planning our wedding has been very exciting for me and Kallie. I have taken the time to prepare him for what is to come. In my culture, when a man comes to marry one of our women, he is expected to pay dowry, dress in our traditional clothes and also prostrate on the floor before the elders of the family. I even showed him videos of other traditional weddings on YouTube to prepare him. Kallie took it all in like a champ and even prepared his family too. It is like a whole performance at an African wedding. Good thing Kallie is open to trying new things and doesn't think it is weird. I never thought that I would be open to a very public wedding and I still am not but I'm happy to have my pictures in National style magazines.

EPILOGUE

ONYECHE

Our wedding was amazing. Kallie and his family were a great sport. They played along nicely and we had a blast. My parents were happy to meet Kallie and they made sure Kallie paid a big dowry. Apparently Kia had told them that Kallie was a millionaire superstar who could afford their extravagant dowry. They determined not to spare him because after all, that might be the only time they ever asked him for money.

I noticed Kia and Roger getting cozy at my wedding. Everyone had a great time and it made my day. Having boundaries is great, especially when it comes to family. Now more than ever, I see the importance of boundaries between my family(this new union with Kallie) and my paternal and maternal family. They made it clear that their interest is really financial and so long as they get money from me, they are happy with me. I have decided that such a relationship is unhealthy and I made it clear to them that I love them but won't be used by them anymore. It is crazy to me that they only call when they need something from me. Couldn't they at least call to check on me without asking for anything?

Seemed like my concerns fell on deaf ears because they responded by calling me a stingy and an ungrateful person. They could call me whatever they wanted to, I don't care. Having Kallie lavishly love me and my kids just makes me so grateful for where I am in my life right now.

After our traditional wedding, Kallie, the kids, our guests and I flew back to the United States late that night. We dropped off the kids with Kallie's parents the next day. They'd offered to watch them for two weeks while we were away for our honeymoon. I didn't know how to feel about that because the kids have always been with me but I tried my hardest not to worry too much and Kallie helped make sure I didn't worry. He kept reassuring me that the kids would be fine with his parents. I believed him because I have seen how they are with the kids. They care about these kids and it is apparent in their actions.

KALLIE

Hello wifey, are you ready for me to show you my bedroom skills?

"I sure am, hubby. How has it been for you to wait this long to taste the cookie?"

It has been worth it for me babe but has not been easy at all.

"I know, it has not been easy for me either. I've wanted to jump you when we first spent time together in your hotel room, back in San Diego and many times after that," she confessed.

You are so beautiful and I want to taste you from head to toe. If that is okay with you. "That's totally fine baby, as long as you let me taste you too, from head to toe. But first, I need you to get me out of my clothes," she responded.

I walked over to her and began to help her out of her wedding dress and something happened when I started undressing her. Our need for each other suddenly took over us.

We couldn't wait to be connected to each other. She turned around and looked at me with fire in her beautiful brown eyes and asked me to kiss her. I didn't wait for her to ask again. When our lips touched, it was a different level of kiss. I got chills and so did she. In this moment, we could finally allow our need for each other consume us without trying to control it. My dick was ready to taste her but I was not trying to lose control before I could show her how long I could last either. She kissed me deeply and sucked my tongue and I could feel her hand making its way to my dick. She grabbed my dick and began to stroke it.

"You have got a good size on you boy. Your dick will fill me up and I can't wait," she said with a hearse voice.

I am happy you like my size. Mmm baby, I like how you are stroking my dick, I said trying not to cum.

"Babe, can I undress you?"

Sure, you can. She helped me out of my shirt and pants.

"Lay down on your back for me," she commanded.

I lay down and she finished taking off her clothes and leaned over me. She started by kissing me deeply while her warm beautiful naked brown skin pressed and slid up and down mine. Next she started kissing my face and it felt good.

Babe, can I take over from here?

"No, just relax and let me treat you. I promise I'll let you treat me or feast on me when I'm done. Although, I doubt that you will still have the energy when I'm done with you, babe," she added.

Okay, keep going. I'm enjoying this babe.

She moved to my neck and then worked her way to my dick. She licked it like she was licking an ice cream cone and it was a very intense sensation.

Babe, I'm about to explode. Can you stop for a second so I don't disgrace my manhood by cumming?

"No, can I ride you right now? I don't want you to feel like you have to prove a point to me on our first time making love," she advised.

Okay, as long as it doesn't bother you if I don't last. She took me in her mouth until my dick was slick with her saliva. I was holding on for her to sit on me before I let go. When she finally sat on my dick, I couldn't control the urge to start pounding her. She sat down gently and started slowly and then her feelings intensified and she started riding my dick faster but still not as fast as I wanted to go. Though she was riding me so well, I couldn't let her keep going. I had to take charge and show her who the real boss was. I rolled her over and she followed my lead. Then she got on her hands and knees, with her behind right in front of my dick and then she said to me;

"I need you to give it to me hard and fast right now."

That was all she had to say to get the beast in me ready to pounce. I was all about satisfying her with my body and moving at the pace she leads but after that command, I let loose. I went fast and hard at my lady's command and made sure I pleased her.

"Damn Kallie, you are good. Keep going at this pace and you are going to make me cum," she said.

I lost control when she started rolling her waist while pushing against me. I came hard and I think I got her pregnant from the amount of juice I spilled into her.

"Damn, that was really good. I didn't think you had it in you, boy," she teased.

There's more where that came from, I promise.

We lay there holding on to each other for about ten minutes. Enjoying the intimacy between us and how amazing it felt to not have to hold off our sexual urges anymore.

"How does it feel to finally taste my cookie?"

It feels amazing and about damn time I did. I will be fucking you everyday for the next two weeks and the rest of our lives after that.

"Hahaha babe, this is more than just a fuck, it is lovemaking and I love you baby.

I am so happy to be sharing this life with you," she added.

I love you too and love hearing you say that you love me. I think I said it like a hundred times to you before you ever said it back to me. You had me feeling insecure for a while there and I never feel insecure.

"Haha babe, I don't believe the great Kallie can ever be made to feel insecure by anyone."

Well, neither did I, until you came along and captured me with your charming sexy self.
Would you like to shower together?
"Sure, babe."
We headed for the shower together and were soon ready for another round of steamy lovemaking in the bathroom. She took the washcloth in her hand and started washing me and when she got to my dick, she stroked a little longer with the washcloth wrapped around my manhood. That drove me crazy and got me turned on for another round. I asked her to turn around and place her hands on the bathroom wall. When she did, she also spread her legs and I stepped between them. She was already wet and sleek; ready for me to plunge into her.

When I connected our bodies, it went wild from there. She felt so right and worth the wait. It was an intense quickie and it was really good.

"Damn boy, mmm I just need to go and lay down because I definitely feel like you just planted your seed in me with that one," she said.

We finished our shower, ordered some room service, ate and went to bed.

Life has taken on a new meaning for me and I couldn't be more grateful for it. Since the first day I met my girl and kids, I knew that my prayers for a family had been answered.
Nine months after the first time we made love, we welcomed a new addition to the family. Our son; Ozudu, was born on my birthday and it couldn't have been a more perfect day for me. I have since adopted Oiza and Oremeyi and they have my name. Life has been so amazing with my wife. I didn't think being married would be this amazing. My wife is an amazing woman and she is crazy about me and our family. I couldn't have asked for a better woman in my life. Of course the media have their opinion about our family but none of that bothers me or my woman. Having a family of my own is even way better than I thought. Life is good.

THE END...

BOOKS BY THIS AUTHOR

Two Worlds, One Heart

Ozohu Saliu lives in the village with her family. She is the oldest of 6 children. Being the oldest female child, she was responsible for raising her siblings. Ozohu has never runaway from her chores and is a dependable person. However, regardless of how hard she tries, her family doesn't show her any respect. Her siblings had better clothes than her and no one expected anything worthwhile of her. Ozohu had to find a way to love and accept herself in spite of the rejection of her family. While all the single women in the village busied themselves in trying to win the proposal of the promising bachelors in the village, Ozohu was busy having dreams of a man like none of the men in her village. She soon found a place she could go to, where her life is perfect and she had the opportunity to be all that she aspired to be without hate.Jay Gordon is a pro basketball player who lives in Long Beach California. Jay loves African women and dreams of marrying an African Queen one day. Jay has had many dream encounters with a specific African Queen that fills his waking moments.Jay's heart was broken by a woman he thought would be His Queen. She left him for a man who she'd broken up with for sleeping with one of her friends. When she stopped responding to Jay's messages, he had to pay her a visit to find out why she was avoiding him...Will Ozohu's parents and siblings stop hating her? How does her new found safe haven impact her life? How does Jay deal with the heartbreak and does Jay find another Queen who won't break his heart?Find out what happens in this exceptional BWWM romance by Maryam Shumate of BWWM

Love.

Please Stay With Me: Book Two Of Two Worlds, One Heart (The Magnetic Power Of Love Series)

"How can this be real? How could this even be possible? Is someone messing with me right now? How could my dream encounters be embodied in my waking moment?" While Jay was contemplating the whole situation, Ozohu stood up and dusted off her wraparound skirt and adjusted her blouse. "She is gorgeous!" Thought Jay. "She has to be about 5'11 tall and has to weigh about 170. She looks like a runway model or an athlete.

Dear God, please let this be real. I have no clue what's going to happen next but I am ready for how this story, our story unfolds. Her rich, dark brown skin is gorgeous. She looks extra shiny and smooth all the way to her feet. She is perfect for me." Jay analyzed her in his mind.

Now that Ozohu is now in Jay's sight, what does he do with her? What happens now?
Will they begin a physical relationship that captures the moments they spent in that imaginary world they created?
Find out what happens in this exceptional BWWM romance by Maryam Shumate of BWWM Love.

Unshakable Faith: How To Thrive After Losing A Loved One

My name is Maryam Shumate, my heart was broken six years ago after losing my first child to a very rare disease. Doctors told me that there was a chance I carried the genes that would cause me to birth sickly babies and lose them at infancy. This is not a story of heartbreak or crucifixion but one of hope and resurrection.

This is about developing Unshakable Faith and thriving after a loss. Welcome to my world and get ready to engage.

Made in the USA
Columbia, SC
27 December 2021